Jack Vance
The Man in the Cage

Jack Vance

The Man
in the Cage

John Holbrook Vance

Spatterlight Press Signature Series, Volume 23

Copyright © 1960, 2005 by Jack Vance

Published by Spatterlight Press

Cover art by Howard Kistler

ISBN 978-1-61947-137-5

Spatterlight Press LLC

Spatterlight
P R E S S
340 S. Lemon Ave #1916
Walnut, CA 91789

www.jackvance.com

Jack Vance

The Man in the Cage

CHAPTER I

AT NOON ON MARCH NINTH, a dump-truck loaded with coarse gray gravel bumped south through a haze of dust and sunlight. The road, narrow and pot-holed, seemed to cut the visible universe into halves: life on one hand, death on the other. To the right were vistas, areas and masses of verdure, in a thousand sunlit shades of green: feather-green date palms, sea-green tamarisk, truck gardens, plots of emerald alfalfa. To the left spread the desert, hot and dreary, sprinkled with black flints.

Noel Hutson drove the truck, a fair-skinned young man with mouse-brown hair, a rather dandified mustache, a tolerant happy-go-lucky expression. Beside him, leaning forward on the edge of the seat, sat Habdid el Kazim, square-faced, narrow-eyed, thick-set and powerful. A curious thin beak of a nose protruded from otherwise flat features; black stubble blurred the lower half of his face. He wore a homespun brown djellaba with the hood thrown back, and at his hip hung a dagger, with a silver-inlaid handle in a silver scabbard shaped like a fish-hook.

The two men had been riding together for fourteen hours, accepting each other's presence with neither hostility nor cordiality. Habdid el Kazim spoke a hundred words of English; Noel Hutson knew a single word of Arabic: *la*, which meant 'no'. Neither knew the other's name.

The road presently swung into the palm grove. After a mile Habdid el Kazim jerked up his hand: "Slow." He looked up and down the road: no vehicles in sight. He pointed. "Turn through there."

Noel twisted the steering wheel. The truck lurched into the shallow roadside ditch, groaned up the hummock opposite, scraped between a pair of palm trees. El Kazim indicated a track leading off across a carpet

of rank salt grass. In low gear they rumbled through the grove, past irrigation ditches, low walls of adobe brick, thickets of tamarisk. Palms of random size and character rose over them, some tall and lordly, others squat, with great unruly heads; most erect, a few twisted and leaning.

El Kazim sat rigid on the edge of the seat. Once, when the wheels slid in mud, Noel gunned the motor: el Kazim made an urgent motion. "The French." His face split in a nervous grin, showing a row of gold teeth. He pointed through the trees. "Two kilometers, no more. Soldiers."

Noel thereafter drove as quietly as possible. The trees thinned; ahead appeared a typical kasbah of the region, a village behind walls thirty feet high, with corner watchtowers, a heavy timber gate. El Kazim motioned Noel to a halt and jumped to the ground. Beside the track stood a sentry; the two conferred. The sentry spoke into an army-type field telephone, listened, gave a signal to proceed. El Kazim climbed back into the cab, jabbed his forefinger toward the kasbah. "We must go fast."

Noel worked the balky gearshift: compound-low, low, second; the Diesel roared and chattered. El Kazim fluttered his fingers nervously. "Fast, fast." Noel thrust his foot down on the accelerator; the truck roared along the road. The timber gate opened, the truck entered a large compound, the gate swung shut.

Noel brought the truck to a smart halt, switched off the engine. He opened the door, stepped out on the running-board. Sunlight stung his damp skin. Three- and four-story mud dwellings, similar to the pueblos of Arizona, surrounded the courtyard — masses of rectangular blocks and planes, penetrated by tunnel-like passages. A caravan had either just arrived or was about to leave: across the courtyard stood a dozen camels, with nearby a heap of saddles, panniers, ropes and straps. An odor of urine, decay, wet straw and smoke of smouldering fires filled the courtyard. Noel pursed his lips in distaste, eased back into the shade of the cab.

A number of men and boys wearing ragged smocks approached to stare in fascination. Noel grinned, gave them a debonair salute. They stared as before, making no response. Noel climbed up into the driver's seat, and ignored them.

Habdid el Kazim, crossing the courtyard, had curtly embraced a hard-faced man wearing a smart gray djellaba and a red fez: urban clothes,

as incongruous to the kasbah as Noel's sun-tans. The man in the gray djellaba was slender and fine-boned, taller than the stocky Habdid, but with the same curious thin wedge of a nose, like a parrot's beak. Another man, short, fat, wearing a nondescript uniform, joined them; the three spoke earnestly. The short fat man jerked his head toward one of the larger buildings, discussing someone not in evidence. Both Habdid el Kazim and the man in the gray djellaba shook their heads decisively, and the short fat man nodded in vindication, as if his side of an argument had been upheld.

Noel watched without interest. Habdid el Kazim hardly seemed a romantic figure; the kasbah was no more than a smelly little village. Thirteen more trips — unless Arthur Upshaw rented another truck, or hired another driver. Unlikely, thought Noel. If it weren't for the money... He slumped back against the leatherette cushion, drummed his fingers on the black rim of the steering wheel. Not too much money, in view of what Upshaw would be making. Well, he had had the experience, and that was what counted.

Across the courtyard the three men had reached a decision. The fat little soldier marched forward. He barked orders, clapped his hands. Men and boys swarmed up into the bed of the truck. Noel descended to the ground, leaned against the hot front fender to watch. The gravel was brushed aside; wooden cases strapped with metal bands were tilted up on end, slid to the ground. At once they were attacked and broken open. The little officer bellowed in anger, herded his crew back to work.

The truck was presently free of its cargo. There were ten crates containing two thousand Mauser pistols, each in a cardboard box complete with trilingual instruction booklet, flask of oil and bristle brush; twenty-four crates of submachine guns, sealed in transparent plastic sacks, six to the crate; thirty cases of nine-millimeter ammunition.

Now, in spite of the officer's expostulations, the group fell on the crates like wolves tearing at a carcass. Noel's interest became revulsion. He shifted his gaze, reassuring himself with reasonable and well-tried assertions. If I don't earn the easy money, someone else will. If the French have a right to weapons, so do the Algerians. He leaned nonchalantly on the fender, cleaning his fingernails with a straw.

The tribesmen swarmed around the crates. They waved aloft the pistols, shouting and calling to each other, tucking one and sometimes two into their ragged garments. The fat man in the army uniform stalked forward and back, calling futile orders which no one heeded. Noel watched the scene with amused detachment: none of his business, he merely drove the truck. He examined his fingernails, which were now clean. His detachment wore thin. He darted a frowning glance across the courtyard. In Tangier a truckload of weapons was a romantic abstraction, symbolic of adventure and excitement. Some day, in circles far removed, he could hark idly back to "the time I worked running guns out of Tangier. Drove south through Morocco, back of the Atlas, out to a little desert fort on the Algerian border…" But now the guns were visible, ugly and black, ready to be discharged into the bodies of young Frenchmen. Noel turned away. Thirteen more loads? Not for me. He climbed sourly back into the cab, displeased with himself, anxious to depart.

Something had changed. The babble in the courtyard quieted. Noel looked around. A tall old man in a white djellaba had appeared. He wore a white turban; a jeweled dagger hung at his waist. His eyes were bright gray, his features lean and austere. He gazed at the plundered crates, called out wrathfully. The babble in the courtyard died completely. The sheikh — such he evidently was — spoke again, holding up his clenched fist. Sullenly, with foot-dragging reluctance, the tribesmen sidled close to the crates. Furtive hands went into garments, came out holding pistols. The short man in the uniform busily stowed the guns back into the crates; the men and boys of the kasbah backed away, glum with disappointment.

The patriarch watched grimly. He gave another order; Habdid el Kazim and the man in the gray djellaba turned about sharply. The little soldier stared in new annoyance.

The patriarch was obeyed. Men went into the building, brought forth four cardboard cartons, which they carried to the rear of the truck. The round-faced man in uniform ran forward, protesting. The patriarch made a small gesture; the soldier's voice broke off in mid-sentence. Two men climbed up into the bed of the truck; the cartons were handed up.

Noel jumped out of the cab, stepped up on the frame, looked back into the bed. The cartons, according to the red and blue label, contained soap powder. Soap? Disconcerting. Awkward. Highly awkward. Noel called across the courtyard to the sheikh. "What's this? I don't know anything about this stuff."

No one heeded him. Habdid el Kazim and the man in the gray djellaba both were voicing vehement objections. The sheikh listened impassively. When they had finished he spoke a curt sentence. The discussion was closed. Habdid el Kazim and the man in the gray djellaba abruptly turned away, walked out into the courtyard. They spoke together for several minutes, glowering toward the sheikh. Habdid el Kazim threw up his hands in fatalistic acceptance of the situation. He patted the man in the gray djellaba on the cheek, strode across the courtyard to the truck. He climbed in the cab. "We go now, back to Tangier."

Noel jerked his head toward the rear of the cab. "What are we carrying?"

Habdid el Kazim turned his head, inspected Noel as if seeing him for the first time. Noel forced himself to meet the glitter of the eyes. Habdid el Kazim settled himself in the seat, made a circling motion with his hand. "Turn the truck."

Grumbling under his breath Noel started the motor, backed up with a jerk, cut the truck around in vicious swerves that expressed his frustration. He was anxious to leave the hot and foul-smelling kasbah. But the four cases of — soap?

The gate swung open; Habdid el Kazim thrust his forefinger ahead. "We go. Fast."

Noel hesitated. It had to be now. Now or never… But what could he do? He raced the motor, let it idle, looked angrily sidewise at Habdid el Kazim. "I don't drive unless I know what I'm driving."

Habdid el Kazim looked at him in surly surprise.

"I'm working for Arthur Upshaw," declared Noel. "He said nothing about a return load."

Habdid el Kazim pointed ahead. "We take to Arthur Upshaw. Fast now, until to the trees. The French are close."

Noel irresolutely shifted into low, engaged the clutch. "Faster, faster!" grated el Kazim. From inside his djellaba he pulled one of the

Mauser pistols. Out the gate the truck rolled, bouncing and rattling across the open space. El Kazim snapped out the magazine, charged it with cartridges.

They gained the shelter of the palms; el Kazim waved his hand to the sentry, motioned Noel to proceed. "Now, back to Tangier."

Noel shook his head sulkily. "I've been driving all night, I'm tired."

"We must go to Tangier. It is necessary."

Noel jammed down the accelerator; the truck careened through the palms. El Kazim braced himself in the seat, half-grinning, half-scowling, the gold teeth shining through his lips.

Fifty yards short of the intersection el Kazim ordered a halt. He went ahead to look up and down the road. Noel stepped out on the running-board, climbed up on the frame, studied the four cartons. If they were what he thought they were — but what else could they be? Contraband for the Algerian rebels normally traveled by caravan, safe from French interception; these cartons of 'soap', originating in Egypt, were probably still warm from the camel's back. And, if they were what he thought they were, they represented a great deal of money. El Kazim whistled. Noel looked around. El Kazim beckoned him forward. Noel swung into the cab, shifted into low gear. The truck lurched forward. El Kazim swung aboard; they turned out into the road.

For an hour they drove north. Neither man spoke. The road ran beside the palm groves, then slanted up among red sandstone bluffs, to strike out across the desert. Noel's eyes drooped with fatigue. He blinked resentfully. After driving all night and most of the day, another fourteen hours on the road was out of the question! And the four cartons of 'soap'! They stuck in his mind, pressed on his nerves. Certain things just weren't done. Noel considered himself an adventurer, a man of gallantry and savoir-faire. Smuggling, gun-running — such affairs carried a cachet of glamour and dash; he collected escapades of this sort as a high-school girl strings ornaments on her charm bracelet. The cartons labeled 'soap' represented something else again, something sordid and disreputable. Involvement would befoul Noel's ego-image, the blurred synthesis of Errol Flynn and Cary Grant he had worked so carefully to build.

A few miles ahead lay Erfoud, a town with a good hotel. It was only reasonable that they should stop to rest. He would telephone to Arthur

Upshaw at Tangier, who could come drive his own blasted truck. Noel cleared his throat. "We're stopping in Erfoud, at the Gîte d'Etape. I've driven enough for one day."

"No, no," said el Kazim shortly. "We must go to Tangier."

"What's the rush?" Noel asked peevishly.

"There is a mistake. The sheikh is old man, he's afraid the French will come. He says we must take the boxes to Tangier. It is a mistake, but now we must do."

"There's not all that rush," Noel grumbled. "I'm too tired to drive. And I don't know about taking those packages. What's in them?"

Habdid el Kazim squinted sidewise at him. "It goes to Tangier."

"I'm not driving to Tangier today," said Noel, looking ahead down the road to avoid meeting el Kazim's angry stare. "I'm in charge of this rig, and I'm not trucking any cargo until I know what I've got." The idea, so expressed, infuriated him. They took him for a simple-minded truck driver, an underling! He jammed on the brakes; el Kazim made a hoarse exclamation of annoyance.

"No, we must not stop! The French will come."

"What's in the cartons?"

"It is not for you!" cried el Kazim. "Go on!"

It was a mistake, a misunderstanding. Sobbing and gasping, Noel stared down at the blood-smeared face. It had happened so fast, with such dreadful finality — why had el Kazim brandished the gun? Noel had struck down his arm; with frantic suddenness they were fighting. Noel had thrust his shoulder under el Kazim's chin, banged the sun-darkened temple against the door frame. He twisted at the gun, saw el Kazim's thumb working at the safety, his forefinger squeezing at the trigger. Noel wrenched the barrel down against el Kazim's wrist; el Kazim's fingers loosened, the gun dangled, then dropped to the seat. Grunting, el Kazim clawed for his dagger; steel whirred free. Before it had been a scuffle; now the issue was life or death.

Noel ground his forearm into el Kazim's neck, held him back against the door, seized the wrist with the dagger. El Kazim rasped through his constricted throat; Noel fought with hysterical strength, too intent to feel fear. El Kazim doubled up his knees, buffeted Noel back. Noel had el Kazim's wrist under his arm; the effect of the kick jerked el Kazim around, down off the seat, where he thrashed arms and legs to recover himself. He lunged, the dagger slashed an inch past Noel's throat. Noel seized the gun by the barrel, beat him on the forehead. Blood squirted down the dark face, between the eyes, down each side of the nose, an awful sight. Noel screamed, struck again and again. He saw el Kazim's eyes staring; they seemed accusing and stern. Noel cried out in agony, struck as hard as he could, to drive away the ghastly sight. The skull broke, the metal sank into something yielding. The head twisted, the mouth wrenched and gaped.

Noel groped open the door, tottered out on the road. He looked down at the bloody gun, at his bloody hands. He flung the gun desperately away, thrust his hands into the sand at the side of the road, rubbed and scrubbed till only a dark dirty stain remained.

Beside him the Diesel engine throbbed and ticked. A car appeared down the road, approached, passed; dark eyes under a white hood flashed incuriously. The car was gone in a pillar of rising brown dust.

Noel took deep breaths. If never before, he must think sensibly. This was adventure, and he didn't like it.

First he must dispose of the corpse. But not here. There was no concealment; it would be found quickly and the UAR, or FLN — whatever they called themselves — would come for him. He climbed up into the cab. Gingerly moving the sprawled shape out of the way, he shifted into low. The truck moved forward.

Ten minutes later the road zigzagged down through sandstone bluffs toward the floor of the valley. Noel stopped beside a deep gulch, opened the door, pulled the body out. It slid and tumbled through the dust, djellaba flapping, until half-way down it caught against a straggling bush. Noel backed down the slope, thrust with his foot; it rolled almost to the bottom. He kicked fragments of rusty sandstone after, and now it was almost invisible. The sound of a motor in the distance? Noel clawed his way back up to the road, jumped into the cab, drove hurriedly away.

A mile farther on he stopped, scooped sand into the cab, scrubbed and swept until the blood stains were one with the rust and grease of years.

He drove slowly north through the palm grove, fretting over a dozen unsatisfactory plans of action. Police? Flight? Tangier? Casablanca? The cartons gnawed at his nerves; what a relief if he could pitch them off into a ditch. But other considerations intervened: those of his personal safety. He had stumbled into this frightening mess; now he must contrive to evade the consequences.

Through the palms appeared a high biscuit-colored wall which marked the outskirts of Erfoud. He drove beside the wall until he reached a crossroads. He paused, looked first one direction, then the other. The main road to Meknes and Tangier stretched ahead. To the right, through a tall Moorish arch, a street led into the French settlement and business district. A side road to the left wound through the palms toward an imposing building on a hill a half-mile distant. This was the Gîte d'Etape, a regional staging hotel built in preparation for tourists who so far had avoided this remote corner of Morocco.

Noel rubbed his face. If he tried to drive through to Tangier he'd kill himself. And the cartons. Why should he do Arthur Upshaw's dirty work? At the hotel he would telephone Tangier. Arthur Upshaw could drive south, or Duff. It was their mess, let them take care of it. Noel wrenched the steering wheel, sent the truck lumbering through the palm grove to the hotel.

He parked in a graveled area near the front entrance, took his jacket and zipper bag from behind the seat, descended to the ground.

A page in a red uniform opened plate-glass doors with ceremony. Noel entered a marble lobby of astonishing amplitude. The floor glowed with Berber rugs; leather armchairs surrounded embossed copper cocktail tables. The far corner of the lobby was given to a bar; here a white-coated bartender polished glassware. The desk clerk stood poised behind the marble registration counter. The three men, all apparently French, watched Noel silently. The lobby was otherwise empty.

Noel went to the desk, produced his passport and was assigned a room. With the guidance of the page, he garaged the truck, then went to his room, showered, changed into fresh clothes.

He lay on the bed, dozed, drifted off into uneasy sleep.

The telephone, ringing in short sharp jingles, awakened him. "Yes?" he muttered.

"Do you want dinner, sir?" inquired a heavily accented voice. It was not the desk clerk, who spoke careful, if pedantic, English.

"Yes," said Noel thickly. "Just a minute." He looked at his watch. Seven-thirty. Arthur Upshaw might be at his apartment by now. "I want to make a call to Tangier."

"Very well, sir. What number?"

Noel gave the number. The line hummed, buzzed; ghost-voices whispered. A man spoke: "Hotel Balmoral."

The long-distance operator turned the line over to Noel. "Is Mr. Upshaw in?" Noel asked.

"No, sir."

"Do you know where I can call him?"

"No, sir. Will you leave a message?"

"No," said Noel shortly, and hung up.

He went down to the lobby, which still was empty. Crossing to the bar, he ordered a highball, took it to one of the deep leather chairs, and sat looking across the expanse of barbaric rugs.

Presently he rose to his feet, went to the desk. The clerk, now back on duty, was chewing a toothpick which he hastily discarded. "I want to make a call to Tangier."

"Yes, sir," said the clerk. "Will you take it here?"

Noel looked about him. "Is there a booth?"

"No, sir. Only this desk telephone."

"It'll do." Noel consulted his address book, read a number to the clerk, who went to the switchboard, put the call through.

The clerk watched with covert interest. American, hence rich, yet he drives up in a truck and wears rough workman's clothes. Bizarre! Certainly not a tourist…There was a wait. A far bell rang again and again. The clerk shook his head. "There is no answer, sir."

"Confound it," muttered Noel. He pondered, flipped to another page in his address book. "Try this number." He read the number to the desk clerk.

The connection was made. The desk clerk shuffled papers with ostentatious disregard for the conversation.

"Hello? This is Noel Hutson. Is Arthur Upshaw available?"

There was a pause.

"Or I'll speak to Duff, if he happens to be there."

Another pause. Noel waited impatiently.

"Damn. Do you know where they are?…Well, give Arthur this message, will you? It's urgent, so make sure he gets it. Okay?…Good. Tell him I'm resigning. Tell him his friends gave me a shipment I don't plan to haul, for him or for anybody else. Tell him if he wants it to come for it himself."

Pause, while Noel listened.

"I don't like to say, not over the phone. Arthur will know. It's business I don't plan to get involved in."

Bizarre and more bizarre, thought the desk clerk.

Noel was describing his whereabouts to the person at the other end of the wire. "…at the Gîte d'Etape. If I don't hear from him I'll throw the stuff in a ditch, and come back to Tangier on the bus."

Pause.

"Right. Also, if you don't see Arthur, will you make sure that Aktouf gets the message? Thanks very much."

Noel hung up the receiver. So much for that. The issues were now resolved. He felt rather pleased with himself.

He sauntered into the dining room. Chandeliers twinkled; glass and silver glittered on crisp table linen. Noel was the solitary diner. Two waiters and a bus boy served him while the head waiter stood a little apart, hands clasped behind his back. Noel seemed to be the only guest in the hotel.

Returning to the lobby he bought an air-letter form at the desk, took it to a chair, and using a late copy of *London Illustrated News* for a pad, wrote:

> *Dear Dad:*
>
> *Trouble has caught up with me and I've got to yell for help. It's a long story which I won't go into, except to admit that, as the family has long maintained, I'm a prize dunce, and half a rascal. But only half. I had to back out. There are some things I can't bring myself to do. I've just now put a message through to my boss, told him I'm quitting. More than anything in the world I want to come back home and start a civilized*

life — anything, so long as it's peaceful and dull. I need a thousand dollars, to settle a few bills and buy a ticket home. I promise you'll never have to worry about me again. Wire the money care of the Lombard Bank at Tangier. I'll collect if and when I get there.

Noel paused in his writing, chewed on the end of his fountain pen. He rose, went to the desk. "What time does the morning bus leave for Tangier?"

"There's nothing direct, sir, you'd have to change at Meknes. The early bus for Meknes leaves at eight."

Noel nodded. "I want to be called at six."

"Very good, sir. Six o'clock."

Noel returned to the chair, resumed his letter.

I just figured a way to copper my bets, and I'm safe as far as Tangier. I may have to do some fast talking — but I won't go into that. I'll see you in a week or so, and give you the whole story.

Noel stopped, thought a moment, then, with a brave flourish of his pen, continued:

Love to Mother, Molly, Darrell and yourself. See you all soon — I hope.

Noel

He folded the letter, sealed and addressed it to: R. M. Hutson, 625 Berry Farm Road, Everton, Pennsylvania. He took it to the desk, dropped it in the mailbox.

He went to his room, locked the door, undressed and went to bed.

His mind raced; sleep was slow in coming. A picture returned again and again to his mind: a stubble-bearded face, the eyes stern and bewildered, blood streaming in a black net over the nose. Then the final crushing blow, the eyes slowly closing, the mouth loose and askew.

Noel moaned softly, covered his head with his hands. "It wasn't my fault," he told himself, "I only did what was right!"

Finally he went to sleep.

✳

At six o'clock in the morning the telephone rang. Noel, already awake and staring at the ceiling, acknowledged the call. With a mumble of glum curses, he swung himself out of bed.

He looked out the window. The morning sunlight was golden and clear; the palms trembled and swayed in the morning air. All serene.

Noel dressed, assuring himself that the situation, though delicate, was still not critical. A day or two must elapse before the FLN — whoever they were — could know that Habdid el Kazim was missing. In the meantime Noel would have returned to Tangier, have made forwarding arrangements with the Lombard Bank, and be safely out of reach in Málaga or Lisbon.

Nevertheless, descending the broad marble stairs, Noel went furtively, and scrutinized the lobby before showing himself.

The clerk who had been on duty the previous evening bade Noel a punctilious good morning. "Will you have breakfast, sir?"

Noel hesitated. By this time Arthur Upshaw should have received his message. Why had he not called back?

The hell with Arthur Upshaw. "No breakfast; I'm rather in a hurry. May I have my bill?"

The page was not yet on duty; the clerk left his desk to unlock the garage.

The cartons of 'soap' were as Noel had left them. He started the truck, backed out and around, set off down the neat black-top driveway.

The clerk watched the truck disappear through the palms, shaking his head and smiling, then went back into the cool lobby.

Not long afterward his switchboard flashed and buzzed to an incoming call.

The clerk responded. *"Le Gîte d'Etape d'Erfoud."*

"Je veux parler avec Monsieur Noel Hutson," said a voice. "Mr. Hutson — is he there?"

"I'm sorry, sir," said the clerk. "Mr. Hutson has already checked out, not twenty minutes ago."

There was a brief silence. Then the voice said, "Thank you very much," and rang off.

CHAPTER II

AT NOON ON WEDNESDAY, April ninth, Darrell Hutson, wearing light-gray flannels and carrying an old leather suitcase, stepped out of the airport waiting room. He signaled; a Fiat *petit-taxi*, hardly larger than a wheelbarrow, darted up. The door swung open, Darrell Hutson climbed in.

The driver twisted around. "Where you going? The El Minzah?"

"You speak English? Good. Calle Erasmus, 20. The Hotel de los Dos Continentes."

With a whir of minuscule motor, the cab turned out onto the highway. Darrell Hutson settled back in the seat. He was two years older than Noel, not quite so tall, more compact, and showed nothing of Noel's flair and dash. His hair was black, cropped short; his expression thoughtful, wary; his mouth compressed, almost grim.

A twenty-minute drive took them into Tangier. With no warning the road burst out upon a magnificent view over the sun-drenched crescent of city, with the Strait of Gibraltar and the mountains of Spain beyond. They angled down the hill, past stucco villas flaming with purple and pink bougainvillea, along streets shaded under eucalyptus, acacia and pepper trees; finally came out into the Place de France. A policeman in white helmet and jacket signaled them to a halt. Pedestrians surged in front of them: tourists from Europe, Australia, North and South America; Turks, Egyptians, Persians, Berbers from the Rif. Jews, Sephardim and Ashkenazi; East Asians; Moroccans proud of their wax-pale skins; Indian merchants with bovine eyes and soft mouths; Negroes from France, the United States, Central Africa; native Tangerines.

The taxi driver, a Spaniard who claimed to have lived ten years in

New York, gestured toward the crowd. "The town is dead. Not like old times." Darrell would hear the remark frequently during the next few days. "The stores, they go broke. Before, people come here to buy; now there's Moroccan duty. Prices is high. People come to change money, then they go to Gibraltar to spend."

"I understand there's no more smuggling either."

"Nothing." The taxi driver's voice was disgusted. "Why you think I drive a cab? For my health? When I make some money, I leave." He snapped his fingers over his head.

The policeman signaled with hands and baton; the taxi drove along Boulevard Pasteur, Tangier's commercial center, crowded with banks and booths of money changers. They turned sharply downhill toward the harbor. The buildings became meaner and dingier as they descended: second-class apartment houses, café-bars, shops.

A block above the water-front the driver turned into Calle Erasmus. He drove slowly, searching along the house fronts, stopped with a jerk. "Number 20. Hotel de los Dos Continentes."

The hotel, by no means as impressive as its name, was a narrow three-story building, freshly whitewashed, with red-tiled steps and window boxes bright with geraniums. Darrell alighted, paid off the cab. The door being locked, he rang the bell. A sturdy button-nosed woman of thirty-five appeared, her face pink with exertion. At the sight of Darrell and his suitcase, she tucked lank strings of blonde hair behind her ears. "Yes, come in, please."

Darrell entered a narrow hall, furnished with a plywood registration desk, a bench, a mirror and a calendar. He put down his suitcase. "Noel Hutson lives here, I believe?"

"Yes, yes," said the landlady, already behind the registration desk.

"Is he in now?"

She shook her head; the strings of hair fell loose, she automatically tucked them back in place. "No, he is not here. One month I have not seen him."

Darrell's voice came more sharply than he intended. "A month? An entire month?"

"Yes. One month."

"Do you know where he is?"

"No. He tells me nothing. I do not ask his business."

Darrell took an envelope from his pocket, extracted a crumpled blue air letter. The postmark was smeared and undecipherable. It had been received three weeks ago. Allowing a week in transit — the times corresponded closely enough.

"I'm his brother," said Darrell. "I've just arrived from the United States, and I'm anxious to find him. Do you know where I could look, or whom I could ask?"

The round pink face became stupid and blank. "He worked on a boat. That is all I know."

Darrell turned away, puzzled and annoyed. "May I see his room?" he asked at last. "There might be something there. A note, perhaps."

"There is nothing. But you may see." The landlady took a key, led him up narrow steep stairs. She turned down the hall, stopped by a door. "Number five." She opened the door, motioned Darrell to enter.

The room was clean and sunny, though by no means luxurious. A double bed, covered with a white counterpane, occupied the center of the room. There was an enormous Spanish wardrobe to the right, a marble-topped table to the left. The table was graced by a bedraggled bouquet of acacia blossoms in a pale blue vase, and under the vase were a number of letters. Mrs. Ritterman — so she had introduced herself — murmured an apology, took up the vase of flowers and left the room. Darrell examined the letters. There were two from his father, the contents of which he knew well; two envelopes, one lavender, one green, addressed in two different feminine handwritings; three commercial letters — bills or notices. Neither the lavender nor the green envelope bore a return address; one was postmarked Málaga, the other Casablanca; both were dated toward the end of March.

Mrs. Ritterman returned; Darrell replaced the letters, looked around the room. There seemed to be no clue whatever to Noel's whereabouts. He half-heartedly opened a drawer: he saw socks, handkerchiefs, half a carton of cigarettes, several matchbooks, one of which he brought out. On one face it advertised the Masquerade Bar, Calle Miranda 37; on the other, the Balmoral Hotel, of the same address.

"The Balmoral," asked Darrell, "is it a good hotel?"

Mrs. Ritterman shrugged. "Very dear. Here it is much less, with all comfort. Do you want a room?"

"I don't think so. I haven't made my plans yet. Is Noel's rent paid?"

"He is two weeks overdue."

Darrell brought forth his wallet. "How much does he owe?"

"Two thousand four hundred francs."

Darrell extracted a five-thousand franc note. "Does that cover a month?"

"Ah! Yes! I will give you a receipt."

Darrell opened the wardrobe, looked at Noel's clothes: a gray-green Glen plaid, a blue worsted of a color richer than Darrell would have chosen for himself, two sport coats, several pairs of slacks.

Darrell felt the pockets. "What are you looking for?" Mrs. Ritterman inquired in a voice which had become a trifle brittle.

"Nothing in particular," said Darrell, closing the wardrobe. "Anything to give me a hint as to where he is."

"You should try at the yacht club; that is where he works. He is sometimes gone for several days before."

"But never so long as a month."

"No, never so long as a month."

They left the room. Mrs. Ritterman spoke over her shoulder as they descended the stairs: "One friend of his came to ask." Mrs. Ritterman shook her head tersely at the recollection. "He was angry that I did not know. How should I know? I have my work. I do not follow the lodgers. Let him be angry. He was not nice."

Darrell made a sound of polite commiseration. In the little downstairs lobby he asked, "If Noel comes, will you tell him I've been here?"

"Yes, of course. Where are you staying?"

"I think I'll try the Balmoral — for a night or two, at least. If I change I'll let you know."

"Very well!" said Mrs. Ritterman, annoyed that Darrell should prefer the Balmoral Hotel, sight unseen, to the Hotel de los Dos Continentes. She bustled forward, opened the door. Darrell took his suitcase, started back up the hill. No cabs came past; he walked all the way to the Boulevard Pasteur. Here, while catching his breath, he noticed the front of the Lombard Bank a short distance up the street.

He picked up his suitcase, pushed through the ornate black iron and glass door, went to a counter where a placard read:

INFORMATION

Man spricht Deutsch
On parle français
Si parla italiano
Se habla español
English spoken
Svenska talas

A handsome gray-haired woman came forward. "I'm the brother of Noel Hutson, who has an account with you," said Darrell.

"Yes?" The woman, brisk and noncommittal, spoke with a clipped British intonation.

"A month ago my father paid a thousand dollars into Noel's account, but we've received no acknowledgment. He's not at his hotel, and we're disturbed. I'd like to know if he's been in, if he's made any withdrawals in the last month?"

The gray-haired woman seemed doubtful. "Noel Hutson — isn't he a very fair young man, with a mustache, dusty-brown hair?"

"Yes, that's Noel."

The woman inspected Darrell's black crew cut, his flat cheeks, his wide thin mouth. "You don't resemble him very much."

"No, we're quite different types."

"I wish I had his complexion. But I haven't seen him for some time. Just a minute." She went behind the wicket, consulted the files, then returned. "His account hasn't moved for over two months. Except for your father's deposit, that is to say."

"I see. Thank you very much. If he happens to show himself, will you mention that I've been in?"

"Yes. Where are you staying?"

"The Balmoral — or so I hope."

"The Balmoral? I don't think you'll get in. It's more of a residential hotel. Most tourists, especially Americans, go to the El Minzah."

"Hmm." Darrell considered a moment. "Well, I've already given the Balmoral address to Noel's landlady, so I'd better go there."

"Good luck in your search."

Darrell returned to the street. He hailed a cab and was taken to the Balmoral Hotel: along Boulevard Pasteur to the Place de France, around and up the hill, left into Calle Miranda, to a stop in front of a marble-paneled vestibule with a bronze and glass door. Discreet bronze letters spelled: BALMORAL HOTEL. Darrell glimpsed an extravagantly large chandelier, wide mirrors, elegant furniture. In the same building, a few yards up the street, a façade of dark brown boards rose behind a border of blue-green century plants. Green neon tubing, not at all discreet, announced:

MASQUERADE BAR.

Darrell alighted from the cab, paid the driver.

A bellboy came smartly forth to take Darrell's suitcase. He entered the lobby, and found the atmosphere even more luxurious than it had appeared from the street. The carpet, buttermilk-color, was thick and resilient; the walls were divided between golden-beige marble and plate-glass mirrors, in which the chandelier generated a thousand glittering simulacra of itself. The furniture, confections of gilt and red plush, could loosely be called Louis Quinze. The registration desk, a flight of marble steps, an elevator occupied the far end of the room. A glass door with a gilded grille led into the Masquerade Bar.

Darrell approached the desk. The clerk was a thin young man with well-brushed black hair, a pencil-line mustache. Darrell requested a room with a bath. The clerk, putting his hands behind his back, smiled quietly. "Sorry, sir. There are only suites and apartments here. Now we are full. Across the street is the Hotel Miranda."

"I see. Are you acquainted with Mr. Noel Hutson?"

"I don't know anyone of that name, sir. But I have been here only two weeks; he may have lived here before."

Darrell nodded, turned away. He crossed the street to the Hotel Miranda, and booked a room. Returning to the Balmoral he left his name and address in the event of a message, then walked down the hill, ate a thoughtful lunch in a café on the Place de France.

Noel was missing — this was the basic situation. His landlady had not seen him for a month. Where to look for him? Darrell had small information. Noel had worked on a boat at the yacht harbor; at some time he had visited the Masquerade Bar (since apparently he was not known at the Balmoral Hotel). Darrell unfolded the air letter and reread it. The sinister hints might mean much or nothing; from an early age Noel had enjoyed the trappings of derring-do. In letters home he had maintained the fiction of work on an excursion boat, but Darrell knew that the excursions were stealthy trips through the night to Sicily, the Balearics, the long Spanish coastline, with cargoes of contraband cigarettes. During the past year, with Moroccan customs effective in Tangier, smuggling had dwindled. How had Noel made his living? Judging by the Hotel de los Dos Continentes, he had enjoyed no particular prosperity, but these were questions of no immediate concern. Where was Noel now?

Speculation was pointless till he had more information. Darrell hailed a cab, asked to be taken to the yacht harbor.

The cab descended the hill in zigzags, turned out into an avenue paralleling the beach, presently discharged him at the white concrete office of the Tangier Yacht Club.

Darrell looked along the line of boats. There were all sizes, both sail and power. Many berths were empty and he saw a number of "For Sale" signs. He entered the gear and paint shop at the end of the pier. A bearded man in a nautical cap turned toward him.

Darrell asked, "Do you speak English?"

The bearded man nodded dourly. "I was born in Belfast and given no choice."

"I'm looking for Noel Hutson. Are you acquainted with him by any chance?"

"I know who he is. You're interested in his boat?"

"Does Noel own a boat?"

"Call it a boat. It floats, it's pointed at the foreparts, there's a motor to push it."

"I don't suppose you've seen him lately?"

"I'd like to. The boat's taking water. Either I pump it out or I let it sink. Berth 108, if you're interested, down along the dock."

"Can you tell me someone who might know his whereabouts? I'm his brother; I've just arrived from the States and I can't seem to run him down."

The bearded man grunted without interest. "You might make inquiry of Arthur Upshaw. Seems to me Hutson did a bit of work aboard the *Deirdre*."

"Where can I find Mr. Upshaw?"

"That I don't know, my friend." The man seemed disposed to speak further, but only said, "There's Upshaw's *Deirdre* out there; the big teak job."

Five minutes later Darrell stood looking down at Noel's boat. The bearded man had dealt with it unkindly; nevertheless it was little enough to look at: a stubby hull with a cabin like a telephone booth. Rust streaked the paint; deck seams were open; a pool of oily water glistened in the cockpit. A card tacked to the cabin offered the boat for sale: "Call N. Hutson, Hotel de los Dos Continentes, or harbor master."

Darrell descended a rickety ladder to the float, peered into the cabin. He could see nothing in particular: a pair of unkempt bunks, a Primus, a bucket, the bulky outline of an engine.

Darrell straightened up, stood thinking. The ugly little hulk was not the craft he would have expected Noel to own. Noel selected his possessions for the effect they would produce. Unless — and Darrell smiled cynically. One of Noel's redeeming traits was a stubborn honesty. Without a boat, he could never speak of the "days in Tangier when I did a bit of smuggling — owned my own boat, in fact. Not much to look at, but with a little luck and a following wind I could take a cargo across to Spain …"

The mystery of the boat was solved. Darrell turned away and met the gaze of a Moroccan youth on the dock, a gaze which instantly shifted to the flight of a distant seagull. The youth was beautiful — a faun. Black hair curled over his olive forehead, he had large hazel eyes, a short straight nose, a curving tender mouth. He wore baggy gray slacks, a green and white pull-over, pointed white Moroccan slippers.

Darrell climbed back up on the dock, stood looking down at the boat. The youth approached, smiling winsomely. He was older than Darrell had first supposed — perhaps seventeen or eighteen.

"You want to buy boat?"

Darrell shook his head. "I think not."

"It's a good boat, runs good. Maybe you like to look inside?"

"No," said Darrell. "Not today. I'm looking for the owner."

"You his friend, huh?"

"I'm his brother."

"You his brother?" The youth's voice rose in glad excitement.

Darrell made a cool appraisal of the eager countenance. "Do you know him?"

"Sure! He's my good friend. I try to help him. I sell boat for him."

Darrell continued to search the affable face. The hazel eyes met his own without a flicker. "So you're a friend of my brother."

"Sure!"

"Where is he now?"

The youth made a vague gesture, looked off and away. "He's somewhere. I guess you see him pretty soon, huh?"

"I suppose so."

"I go tell him you here. You want?"

"I certainly do."

The Moroccan lad poised himself. "I go tell him. Where?"

"Where what?"

"Where is Mr. Hutson? I go tell him."

Darrell grinned sadly. "You don't know either. But you'd like to. Does he owe you money?"

The lad's face was blank; apparently he failed to understand.

"Thanks anyway," said Darrell. He sauntered down the dock. A few steps behind came the Moroccan youth.

Darrell found his way to the *Deirdre*, a far cry from Noel's dingy little craft. It was fifty feet long with a powerful black hull, varnished teak decks and cabin.

"That's Mr. Upshaw's yacht," said the Moroccan youth by Darrell's shoulder. "The 'Derder'— that's how they call him. Nice, huh?"

"Yes. Very nice."

"You like to buy?"

"No. Not especially."

"For sale cheap. I like to buy," he told Darrell with a look of confiding candor. "But I don't have money."

Darrell nodded without interest. From aboard the *Deirdre* came sounds of activity.

Darrell asked, "Is Mr. Upshaw aboard now?"

The youth shrugged. "Maybe so. He wants to sell. Mr. Upshaw he's got no more money. He's broke." He giggled playfully. "Noel — he's got lots of money, huh?"

"Noel? Lots of money?" Darrell stared at the youth in surprise. "What makes you say that?"

"He make lots of money. Noel's smart guy. I like to see him." His voice took on a wheedling note. "You tell me where Noel is. I like to see him."

Darrell looked back to the *Deirdre*. "I'd like to see him too."

A young man in tan shorts and striped yellow and white shirt appeared on deck, carrying an aqualung harness with two tanks. He had long legs, burly shoulders, a face rather pale and set, with brooding eyes, a sensitive mouth drooping disdainfully.

Darrell turned to the Moroccan lad. "Is that Mr. Upshaw?"

"Him? That Mr. Duff Mekkinisser. Mr. Upshaw is uncle of him."

Duff climbed up from the float to the dock, shot Darrell a quick cold stare.

"Hello," said Darrell. "You're Mr. Duff Mekkin — Mek-k —"

"McKinstry."

"Oh. McKinstry. I'm looking for Noel Hutson."

Duff laughed bitterly. "You too? What's he done you out of?"

"Nothing, during the last year or two. As a matter of fact I'm his brother."

"His brother, eh?" Duff McKinstry spoke in the rounded accents of the upper-class English. He put down the aqualung equipment, stared fixedly at the young Moroccan, whose smile became glassy. Duff looked back to Darrell. "Then you don't know where Noel is camped out?"

"No," said Darrell. "I've come here looking for him. We had a letter, and it seems to be the last anyone knows of him."

Duff cocked his head in quick interest. "You had a letter?" He swung on the Moroccan youth, spoke in a rush of guttural Arabic, waved his hand. The Moroccan youth, a smile pasted inaccurately over his mouth, sidled away.

Meeting Darrell's puzzled glance, Duff said sharply, "That's Slip-Slip. He's a bad lot. Sneak-thief and worse. Don't get mixed up with him. Let me see the letter," he said gruffly. "There might be something in it which concerns me."

"I think not," Darrell replied politely. "It's a personal letter."

Duff opened his mouth to speak, closed it again. He turned his head at the sound of an automobile approaching along the dock. A black Mercedes-Benz convertible darted close beside them, halted. A girl of eighteen or nineteen, wearing a black turtle-neck sweater, a gray tweed skirt, sat behind the wheel. She was pale, pretty, with a look of wild undisciplined intelligence, and noticeably resembled Duff. But where Duff's eyebrows rose in an arrogant arch, hers were skeptical and supercilious. Duff's mouth drooped in something like petulance; the girl's mouth was wry and reckless.

Duff hoisted the aqualung equipment into the car, jerked his head toward Darrell. "Another Hutson. He's looking for Noel."

"Who isn't?" said the girl without interest.

Duff jumped into the car; she shifted into low. Duff made the briefest of salutes. The motor roared, they were gone.

Darrell stood looking in puzzlement after the diminishing car. The two McKinstrys — the girl was evidently Duff's sister — had been antagonistic, as if Noel had inflicted some serious harm upon them. "What's he done you out of?" Duff had asked. The situation evidently was complicated, but Darrell could not see Noel in the role of a thief or a swindler. Noel was addicted to the flamboyant, the picaresque; he was sometimes irresolute, sometimes irrational, a braggart, a spendthrift, a woman-chaser. But Noel had never been devious, never a thief. Cigarette smuggling, yes, this was a crime which entailed no loss of face. Theft or swindling, no. Noel was very sensitive as to the figure he cut.

But Noel was also missing. If Arthur Upshaw and the McKinstrys were ignorant of Noel's whereabouts, what had happened? Just what was going on? Darrell could envisage a number of possibilities, all dire: illness, death, flight, detention. Another theory could be derived from Noel's notorious weakness for pretty girls: he might be holed up at some nearby resort, heedless of the trouble he was causing.

Darrell set off down the dock. Slip-Slip followed at a discreet distance. Darrell swung around. "What do you want?"

The smile was genial, the face beatific. "You like a guide? I take you through the medina. I show you girls."

"No, thanks."

Slip-Slip became even more affable. "Anything you like, I fix."

"No, thank you." Darrell turned to go then hesitated. "Why are they angry with Noel? What's he done?"

Slip-Slip shook his head. "I don't know." And he added thoughtfully, "Mr. Duff, he's always mad at something."

Once again Darrell turned away. Slip-Slip tugged at his sleeve. "You want to find where Noel is?"

"Naturally."

"You know where is the Masquerade?"

"Yes."

"Many times Noel goes to the Masquerade. Phil — that's his good friend. Maybe he knows."

"Phil?"

"That's right."

Darrell nodded. "If I see him I'll ask." He walked out to the street, hailed a cab, gave the address of his hotel. Slip-Slip stood on the dock, looking after him.

CHAPTER III

CALLE MIRANDA WAS DIM with twilight, at that indistinct time between the color of day and the chiaroscuro of night. The tubing which spelled MASQUERADE shone pallid green, but had not yet become charged with the poisonous crackling brilliance it would assume at midnight.

Darrell went into the Hotel Miranda, obtained a telephone guide. He opened to the U's, ran his finger down the page — *Upshaw, Arthur. Miranda 37. 29-66-42.*

Miranda 37, no problem there. Miranda 37 was the address of the Hotel Balmoral.

Darrell stepped out into the dusk, crossed the street, and for the third time that day entered the marble, gold and red-plush lobby. In one of the straight-backed chairs sat a raw-boned young man wearing reddish-brown slacks and a brown tweed jacket. His face was sunburned to the same color as his trousers, except where a white streak above his ears indicated a recent haircut. He sat cracking his knuckles and tapping the floor, either nervously or impatiently.

The desk clerk with the bony jaw and rat-tail mustache nodded with remote courtesy at Darrell's approach. Darrell said, "I want to speak to Mr. Arthur Upshaw, who lives here, so I understand."

The clerk's manner altered. "Mr. Upshaw is the owner, sir. He is not in. I'll be glad to take a message."

"Mr. Upshaw owns the hotel?"

"Yes, sir. The entire building."

"Well, well," said Darrell thoughtfully. "I'm at the Miranda across the street, as I told you. Will you have him give me a call?"

"With pleasure, sir." The clerk wrote on a pad of forms.

"Perhaps you know where I can get in touch with him now?"

"I believe he's at the old family home on Calle Costanza. If it's an important matter you can call him there."

Darrell nodded. "Where's the telephone?"

"In the booth, sir. I'll put you through."

Darrell entered the booth, heard the whir of a ringing bell, a click. A voice said, "Hallo. Duff McKinstry here."

"This is Darrell Hutson. I'd like to speak to Mr. Upshaw, if it's convenient."

Duff's voice was cool. "I'm afraid it's not really convenient. He's at his accounts and I assume he'll be occupied all evening."

"If he finds that he has a minute to spare, will you ask him to call me? I'm at the Hotel Miranda. It's about my brother —"

"You've had word from Noel?"

"No. I hoped Mr. Upshaw could give me some idea where to look for him."

Duff laughed harshly. "You're barking up the wrong tree, old man. If Arthur knew where to find Noel, he'd be there and so would I."

"I'd still like to talk to Mr. Upshaw."

"I'll give him your message. You say you're at the Miranda?"

"That's right."

"Hmm. Isn't that a bit thick? Just a wee bit?"

"Why?"

"Don't be naïve, old man. We're in a very difficult position, and you don't help, turning up like this. It's just a bit suggestive. We can't afford it."

"I don't know what you're talking about. I'd still like to speak to Mr. Upshaw."

"I'll give him your message."

Darrell hung up and stood fuming. It was unlikely, he thought, that he and Duff McKinstry would ever become close friends. Arthur Upshaw he had never met. Arthur Upshaw might be more reasonable.

Darrell's reflections were disturbed by a girl descending the marble stairs. She was of medium height, supple and loose-limbed, wearing an oyster-white linen suit another woman might have considered a trifle too tight. Silky chestnut hair hung to her shoulders, her pink mouth was twisted up at the corners into an insolent little crook. She looked merry, happy-go-lucky, marvelously beautiful, and Darrell had the puzzling feeling that he had seen her before. The girl joined the bony-faced young man in the sorrel slacks. They left the lobby, she laughing and impulsive, he tongue-tied.

Darrell went to the registration desk. The clerk, divining by professional insight that Darrell had suffered a rebuff, had resumed his austere pose.

Darrell asked, "Who is the young lady who just went out?"

The clerk looked at Darrell from under lofty eyebrows. "One of our residents, sir."

"What is her name?"

"I'm sorry, sir. I'm under strict orders not to —"

But Darrell had already departed, and was pushing through the bronze and glass doors. At the edge of his vision was a swift and furtive motion. Darrell stopped short, peered through the dusk.

Street lights shining through foliage were no aid to the eyesight. They served only to camouflage anyone who might choose to stand in a doorway.

Darrell shrugged. Tangier's reputation as a city of intrigue possibly had warmed his imagination. Possibly. He went to the Masquerade Bar entrance a few yards up the street, walked in.

The interior of the Masquerade Bar was rich with color. Heavy beams supported a rattan-covered ceiling; the walls displayed brass and copper plates, up to a yard in diameter, stamped with intricate arabesques. From the beams hung three large globes — brass lighting fixtures, studded with coin-size lenses of blue, green and red glass. Booths upholstered in red, yellow and green goatskin skirted the front and far side of the room. The bar ran across the rear, with a kitchen behind.

Darrell had come in at a quiet time. Only three of the booths were occupied, only three people sat at the bar — a portly little man in a snuff-brown corduroy suit and two carefully dressed young women: one dark and sleek as a wet otter, with gold rings five inches in diameter hanging from her ears; the other blonde, a trifle overweight, her breasts constricted into the shape of a pair of large Dutch wooden shoes. The three animatedly chaffed and chatted in quick British accents with the bartender.

Darrell took a stool a few places down the bar. The portly little man stared at him critically, then looked away. "American," he said in a voice of mild disappointment. The dark girl puffed a cigarette with lips carefully pursed; the blonde girl arranged her fundament more evenly over the stool.

The bartender came to serve Darrell. No ordinary bartender, he wore a beautiful gray Shetland sport coat, olive-drab flannel slacks. He was tall and sunburned, with a loose dry thatch of silver-blond hair, a long droll mouth, a long chin, eyes the color of quicksilver — unquestionably American. "What'll it be, sir?" he asked.

"A martini, please."

"You've come to the right place," said the bartender. "Right here is martini capital of the world." He occupied himself behind the bar.

"I like Phil because he's so modest," said the blonde girl, voice more than a trifle slurred.

"I'm full of old-fashioned virtues," said Phil the bartender. "A real complex mess."

"I like Phil too," said the dark girl. "He gave me a tip on a horse race once. I lost my chemise, of course. Phil made a pot on a different horse."

"Phil's a deep one," said the portly little man. "There's a bit from Gilbert and Sullivan that deals with men like Phil. What is it now? Something, something…?"

" 'A loaf of bread, a jug of wine,' " sang the blonde girl, who appeared befuddled by drink.

"That fits," said the bartender. "At the end of the week, after paying my bills, that's about what I got left." He set the martini before Darrell, the glass frosted, the liquid sparkling and swimming with light. "Try that, and if you don't like it, we'll just throw it out."

"Oh, don't do that, just pass it down here," said the portly little man. "You can test several before you decide."

"I'm trying to earn an honest living," Phil told Darrell, "but Mr. Burdette wants to turn me out to my creditors."

"You've taken enough of my money to buy the place," said Mr. Burdette.

"I'm proud to have you for a customer, Mr. Burdette. I wish I had more like you." He turned back to Darrell. "How's the martini?"

"Fine... I've been told that you're acquainted with Noel Hutson."

"Sure, I know Noel. Haven't seen him around for some time. I guess he ducked over to Spain to taper off the mad pace."

"Do you know for sure he's gone to Spain?"

Phil looked at him curiously. "Heavens no. I don't know nothing for sure, except water runs downhill and I gotta pay my rent. Rent. That's a bad word." He poured himself a small half-finger of whiskey, added a splash of soda, drank the mixture in a gulp. "How'd you like to be my landlord, Mr. Burdette? Good hotel going cheap."

"No, thanks."

"How about you girls? Tangier's a boom town — so they say."

"Boom is right," said Mr. Burdette. "Flat on its face."

Phil grinned at Darrell. "Mr. Burdette is a seller of high-grade automobiles, in case you need another Rolls or a couple Porsches to run on a leash."

Darrell shook his head. "Not just now. I'm only in town long enough to locate my brother."

"Your brother? Who's he? You mean Noel Hutson's your brother? Well, well, well. Glad to meet you. I'm Phil Beresford."

"Who is Noel Hutson?" asked Mr. Burdette without interest.

"You've seen him a dozen times," said Phil. "Tall nice-looking lad, wears one of them musketeer mustaches."

"Yes, I know who you mean. What's he done?"

"That's a rude question, Mr. Burdette."

"Sorry."

"He's disappeared into thin air," said Darrell. "I've checked everywhere, with everyone. No one knows a thing."

"Well, that's Tangier for you. Wicked city."

"Where everything shuts up at ten o'clock," sniffed the blonde girl. "You call that wicked?"

"It stands to reason," Phil told her. "You can't be wicked with the doors open. At least I can't."

"I'll be wicked any time I want," said the blonde girl carefully and with emphasis.

Darrell somberly drank his martini. Mr. Burdette and the dark girl presently took their leave. The blonde girl remained. She looked toward Darrell, who avoided her gaze. She let herself carefully down off the stool, walked toward the restrooms.

"She's absolutely tanked," remarked Phil admiringly. "You'd hardly know it. Wonderful capacity."

"I'll have another martini," said Darrell. "How about yourself?"

"I never refuse."

Darrell watched while Phil Beresford mixed the drinks. "You know Noel fairly well?"

"From across the bar. Nice lad, never made trouble."

"He wrote a letter home a month ago. It doesn't say much, except that he's in trouble. It must have been about the time he disappeared. What do you suppose happened to him?"

Phil ran a hand through his silver-blond hair, shook his head. "I couldn't say. This place is always full of emergency."

"There must be talk."

"That's where I bow out," said Phil. "I gotta live here."

The blonde girl returned from the restroom. She hoisted herself back up on the bar stool, stared at Darrell with steady intensity.

"She's harmless," muttered Phil, "but don't buy her a drink, unless you want to carry her out."

A middle-aged couple entered, the man in a tweed jacket and knickers, the woman in a tailored suit. They ordered brandy, turned frozen stares first at Darrell, then at the blonde girl.

Phil came back to stand in front of Darrell. "Have you talked to Arthur Upshaw?"

"No. Just Duff McKinstry."

"Duff can't tell you anything. You won't get much more from Upshaw."

"Just what goes on?"

"Oh, high finance, excursions and alarms, just the general run of things." He looked up as the outside door burst open. Into the bar ran the girl in the cream-colored linen suit. Behind her, more sedately, came the raw-boned young man in the red-brown slacks.

Phil saluted the girl with enthusiasm. "Here's T-Bone and her latest beau. Gracious, how you do get around, T-Bone!"

T-Bone came to the bar, took the stool beside Darrell. The young man stood at her shoulder, fidgeting and restless.

The blonde English girl said loudly, "Who left the door open?"

Phil leaned over the bar and stared deep into T-Bone's clear blue eyes. "T-Bone, what did I tell you when I hypnotized you last night?"

T-Bone frowned, pursed her lips. "I forget."

"I said that whenever I snapped my fingers you'd feel the irresistible urge to throw your arms around my neck and kiss me."

"I don't remember that!"

"That's the beauty of hypnotism," said Phil. "Next, when I snapped my fingers twice —"

From the kitchen came a short thick woman in a black dress, walking with a peculiar long slow stride. "Psst," said T-Bone. "Mrs. Phil!"

Looking neither right nor left Mrs. Phil walked quietly along behind the bar. She poured out a bucket of ice cubes, looked over the counter. T-Bone wrinkled her nose. Mrs. Phil walked quietly back the way she had come.

T-Bone jumped down off the stool, flounced over to one of the booths with her young man. Phil Beresford heaved a deep sigh. "You've just witnessed the cross I bear through life," he told Darrell. "T-Bone."

"I have a feeling I've seen her before," Darrell said reflectively. "Where, I don't seem to remember…"

Phil shook his head. "You'd remember."

"As a matter of fact —" Darrell twirled his glass, looked down into the pale vortex. Occasionally Noel, in his letters home, had enclosed photographs. "Is she friendly with Noel?"

"Oh, about like the catnip is friendly with the cat."

"I'm almost sure that Noel sent home a photograph of her and himself on the beach."

"I've seen the picture," said Phil. "In fact I took it. T-Bone modestly wearing a couple of lace handkerchiefs. She drove me near crazy."

A waiter was bending over the booth. T-Bone ordered with expressive gesticulations of hand and wrist.

The blonde called out, "Phil, ducky, serve me a drink, there's a boy."

"Sure! What do you want?"

"A nice Pimms cup, the way I like it."

"We're out of that just now. How about a beer?"

"I'll have a pink gin."

Phil poured grenadine into a dollop of gin, added three maraschino cherries. "There. How's that?"

"Lovely."

Phil sidled back down the bar. "It's the cherries that does it," he told Darrell. "Whenever a fancy drink comes up I invent a new recipe. So long as I'm lavish with cherries, there's no kicks. I even get compliments."

The waiter was serving T-Bone and her escort. Phil watched with a marveling shake of the head. "The way I see it, when the Creator made T-Bone he had one idea in mind, and that was the nicest most alluring piece of female humanity he could think up."

Darrell admitted the felicity of the plan.

"Kinda have to suspect the good Lord of our own human failings," Phil reflected. "'Scuse me if that's blasphemy, I don't mean no offense."

He looked over Darrell's shoulder; his manner changed; he began to wipe the bar with a damp cloth.

Darrell turned to see Duff McKinstry's sister, still wearing her gray skirt, her black turtle-neck sweater, her expression of precocious wisdom and recklessness.

"Hello, Ellen," said Phil diffidently.

Ellen nodded. She looked at Darrell. "You called the house tonight."

"Yes."

"Mr. Upshaw was busy at the time, but he'd like to see you now."

Darrell swiveled around on the stool, sat collecting his thoughts. His mind was fuzzy: three martinis, no dinner. "Very well. Where is he?"

"He's not here. He sent me to pick you up."

Darrell stepped down from the stool. "Let's go."

"Hey!" Phil Beresford called after him. "You was buying me that drink; I wasn't buying for you."

"Oh," said Darrell. "Excuse me." He hurriedly paid his bill.

"That's the margin between profit and loss right there," Phil explained to his customers, as Darrell followed Ellen McKinstry from the bar.

The Mercedes-Benz was parked a few yards down the street. Ellen jumped in; Darrell followed more carefully, and his caution seemed to irritate Ellen. She waited with pointed patience as if he were a person of advanced years who might be startled or injured by too sudden a start. At last he was settled; she flicked the starter, switched on the head-lights. White light reached down the street, picked out a figure leaning against a tree. The face was no more than a pale blur, but the clothes showed distinctly: baggy gray trousers, a green and white pull-over.

The Mercedes-Benz throbbed, swept forward; the figure slipped back out of sight. Darrell looked at Ellen; if she had noticed she said nothing.

Chapter IV

At the bottom of Calle Miranda the Mercedes-Benz swung to the left, rushed up the hill. Darrell braced himself. He asked, "Have you ever killed anybody driving this thing?"

"Not yet." Ellen's voice was flat.

The car swooped over the crest of the hill, veered around a corner. Ellen lifted her foot from the accelerator, fed power half-way through the turn. Darrell gripped the door. White villas fled astern like wisps of cloud behind an airplane.

Darrell slumped into the seat. Ellen seemed bored and lax. Darrell asked, "Do you always drive this way?"

"What way?"

"Idiotically fast."

"Fast?" She made a sound of contempt. "I can do a hundred and thirty in this job."

"I understand why your Uncle Arthur wanted me to come to him. He's ridden with you before."

"No," she said in a voice even chillier than before. "He doesn't dare."

An odd thing to say, thought Darrell. Ellen made no explanation.

They swept along Calle Costanza, a narrow lane cut into the steep hillside and overhung by great masses of foliage, made a hairpin turn that sent gravel flying.

A moment later Ellen said, "You can relax your grip, we're there." She bore down on the wheel; the convertible swerved through a stone archway, spraying up another wake of gravel. Two quick twists, application of brakes, the convertible stood at rest under a stucco portico. Ellen switched off the ignition, jumped to the ground. "This way," she said crisply. "Mind the flower pots. Or kick them over if you care to, it's all the same to me."

Darrell came to life. He opened the door, alighted. Ellen ran up the steps to the porch, turned and waited. Darrell searched her face for any hint of amusement, but found only unconcern. "That was quite an experience," he said thoughtfully.

Ellen opened the door. "This way, please." She led him through a living room, furnished in dark oak and rust-colored leather, into an old-fashioned study. Bookcases occupied two walls; the other two walls were paneled in walnut. The ceiling was white plaster, heavily beamed. Logs blazed in a fireplace, a table supported a lamp with green glass shade. The head of a massive lion, mounted as a trophy, hung over the fireplace.

Back to the fire stood Arthur Upshaw, a man of about fifty, wearing a suit of conservative gray twill. He was tall, heavy-boned, gray-haired, gray-eyed, heavily handsome. He nodded, but made no move to come forward and shake hands. "Mr. Hutson? I'm Arthur Upshaw. Sit down, if you please."

Darrell lowered himself into the corner of a leather couch. Ellen sprawled into a chair nearby, thrust her legs toward the fire, fixed her eyes on Darrell's face.

"A glass of sherry?" asked Upshaw.

"No, thanks."

Upshaw clasped his hands behind his back. "You arrived in Tangier this morning, so I understand."

"That's correct."

The pewter gaze roved Darrell's face. "My nephew tells me that you want to help us locate Noel Hutson."

Darrell started to reply, then checked himself. He said after a moment, "I want to find Noel, certainly. I had hoped that you might know, in a general way at least, where he might be."

"You are his brother, eh?"

"I'm his brother."

"You'll consider this an impertinence, but may I see your passport?"

Darrell handed over the green booklet. Upshaw flipped through one or two pages, returned it. "Thank you. Damned imposition, I know. But I like to be sure with whom I am dealing. Good plan, don't you think?"

"I assume the worst to begin with."

Ellen made a small sound. Arthur Upshaw's eyes widened an eighth of an inch.

"I understand," he said, "that you come in response to a letter from Noel." Elaborately casual, he probed at the fire. Ellen maintained her fixed scrutiny of Darrell's face.

Apparently, thought Darrell, they believe the letter to be of relatively recent date. He saw no reason to disabuse them. "Yes," said Darrell. "Quite true. As a matter of fact, parts of this letter puzzle me." He started to reach into his breast pocket, then checked the motion.

Arthur Upshaw's eyes followed his every move. "Perhaps I'll be able to clear it up."

"Possibly. Of course I'm mainly concerned in finding Noel. Could you tell me the circumstances under which he disappeared? In complete confidence, naturally."

Arthur Upshaw teetered up and down on his toes. "A month ago he set out to perform a certain bit of business for me. He never returned. That's the essence of the situation. This letter of his, do you have it with you?"

Darrell ignored the question. "What I'm getting at, exactly where did Noel disappear? He must have left some sort of trail."

Arthur Upshaw nodded. "We'll get around to that, but I think the letter might possibly be helpful. I wonder if I might see it?"

"It's a personal letter, Mr. Upshaw. I doubt if it would tell you any more than it has me."

From the corner of his eye Darrell became aware that Ellen was grinning, faintly but unmistakably.

Arthur Upshaw poked at the fire. "It's very important that I locate Noel. I don't mind saying that a considerable amount of money is involved. A very considerable amount."

"I understand your concern."

"It seems to me that our interests coincide. I think it's to your advantage to help me as much as possible."

Darrell looked into the fire a moment. "I'm not so sure that our interests coincide. They touch here and there. You want to recover your money. I want to find my brother."

Upshaw made a small impatient gesture; Ellen's grin became wider. Darrell could not decide whether her malice was directed against her uncle or himself. "It's a distinction without a difference," declared Arthur Upshaw. He jabbed at the fire.

"Perhaps I haven't expressed myself well," said Darrell. "I suspect that my brother is in trouble. I'm anxious that we cooperate, but I don't want to rescue your money and leave Noel in the soup."

Arthur Upshaw's eyes were once more riveted on Darrell's face. "You pose a hypothetical and complicated situation. Isn't it easier —"

"It's not complicated," said Darrell. "If you'll answer my questions, I'll show you the letter. It's as simple as that."

Upshaw considered. "What sort of questions?"

"Where did Noel go when he disappeared? Is there a possibility of foul play? Who saw Noel last? Have the police been notified?"

Upshaw selected the last question. "The police have not been notified, for a very good reason. Our conversation is confidential, of course?"

"Certainly."

Upshaw nodded placidly. "I don't mind admitting that upon occasion, like other good people of Tangier, I've helped facilitate trade across artificial international barriers. In short, I am a smuggler. Still a gentleman, I hope."

"I thought smuggling out of Tangier had come to an end."

"To a large extent. Smuggling today is not only unprofitable, it's illegal. Therefore I can hardly take my problems to the Tangier police."

"I can, however."

Upshaw shrugged. "That naturally is at your option."

"Noel was working for you when he disappeared?"

"Yes. I can't take care of the donkey work, nor would I care to."

"But, if smuggling is unprofitable —"

Upshaw held up his hand. "Certain types of operation — regrettably those most flagrantly illegal — still offer opportunities. I won't expatiate for obvious reasons."

"Apparently then, Noel was engaged in a smuggling operation when he disappeared."

"I won't contradict you. Through the incredible stupidity of a certain person, Noel was entrusted with responsibilities far beyond his scope. I am afraid," said Upshaw pompously, "that Noel was tempted by the opportunity."

Darrell ignored the implied accusation. "Where did the operation take Noel?"

Upshaw turned to poke again at the fire. "Isn't that information contained in his letter?"

"Where you sent him and where he wrote this letter might be two different places."

Upshaw turned the full stare of his gray eyes on Darrell. "From where did he send the letter?"

"I don't know. He isn't specific."

Upshaw's shoulders sagged a trifle. "I see."

Ellen asked, "What about the postmark?"

"It's a smear."

Upshaw walked back and forth across the hearth. "This letter — does it mention any landmark, anything which might give a hint as to his whereabouts? I say, Mr. Hutson, wouldn't it be simpler to show me the letter?"

"Simpler for you, Mr. Upshaw."

"If the letter is so innocent, why won't you show it to me?"

"Because it's all I have to bargain with."

Upshaw made an impatient gesture. "Does he make even the slightest reference to his surroundings? I know Morocco well. I might be able to identify an allusion which escapes you."

"It's possible, but there's no such allusion. Where in Morocco did you send him?"

Arthur Upshaw realized that he had allowed himself to reveal a fragment of definite information, and his voice raised in pitch. "Actually, Mr. Hutson, your question is immaterial. He certainly is no longer at this particular place. Under the circumstances I consider it only your duty to show me the letter you received from Noel."

Ellen said in a neutral voice, "It's clear he doesn't intend to, Arthur, so why not change the subject?"

Upshaw turned Darrell so cold a stare that Darrell tensed to duck, should his host decide to swing the poker.

"Damn it," muttered Upshaw, "there's a large sum of money involved. I don't know whether Hutson is alive or dead. I don't really care, if only—"

Darrell nodded. "I mentioned that our interests aren't identical. I want Noel; you want your money."

"The money is enough! I'm severely compromised! You ignore the damages I've sustained. Do you intend to make good your brother's obligations?"

"Perhaps you have grounds for a suit?"

"Naturally not. I'm a smuggler; I've relinquished my claims to legal protection. But there's still a point of honor involved."

"I can't see how it affects me."

"You have a letter from the man who ran off with my property. I want to see it. I have every right to see it."

"I'm not convinced that Noel ran off with your property," said Darrell. "And that changes the whole picture. I know Noel pretty well. For all his faults, he isn't a thief."

Upshaw snorted cynically, "My property and your brother disappeared in very close conjunction. He was a free agent up to the moment of his disappearance. I claim, and any reasonable man would agree, that Noel stole my property!"

"Consider me unreasonable, if you like," said Darrell.

Upshaw shrugged in defeat; Ellen stared at Darrell in something like fascination.

"Exactly what is this missing property?" Darrell asked.

"That's beside the point. You should feel an obligation to show me that letter."

"I don't believe it would help you, Mr. Upshaw. That's my honest opinion. Why can't you do things my way? We'd both profit if I knew where to start looking for Noel."

Upshaw slowly shook his head, as if straining for patience. "My nephew and I have made exhaustive inquiries. During the last month we have traveled everywhere in Morocco; we have hired agents in Casablanca and in Spain. Do you think you can succeed where we have failed?"

"I don't know till I try."

"Do you speak French?"

"Very little."

"We do. Do you speak Arabic?"

"None whatever."

"We are both quite fluent. Do you know the details of this business, the people involved, the Moorish mentality, the officials who have been bribed, those who have not?"

"Naturally not. But I've got to look; it's my duty. The rest of my life I'd never feel easy if I made no attempt to find Noel, and you seem to be the logical man to come to for information."

Ellen, her face a mask of absolute boredom, rose to her feet, sauntered from the room.

"You have offended Ellen," said Arthur Upshaw gravely.

"I have?"

Arthur Upshaw held up his hand. "Please don't apologize; I do the same thing continually. She is disgusted by any reference to honor, faith or duty; she experiences physical nausea at the mention of altruism, chivalry — virtue of any kind, in fact. She is not yet twenty years old, but she affects the cynical wisdom of a strip-tease dancer." And he prodded viciously at the fire.

Darrell watched him with curiosity; he spoke with a deeper and more bitter emotion than the topic seemed to merit. Upshaw, as if reaching a decision, put down the poker, turned, clasped his hands behind his back, gazed pontifically at the ceiling. "There seems no point continuing the discussion. You state that this letter is of a personal nature. I am forced to take you at your word. Indeed, if it were otherwise, you would not be here, but out seeking Noel at whatever address he might have mentioned."

Darrell rose to his feet. "Please don't bother to call Ellen. I prefer walking."

Upshaw started to speak, then rubbed his chin. "Just as you please, Mr. Hutson." He conducted Darrell to the front door, bade him good night.

Darrell walked down the driveway, out into Calle Costanza. Before him spread the twinkling lights of the city. He turned east, sauntered downhill along the winding street.

The evening had yielded no information to speak of. Nothing from the Masquerade Bar, very little more from Arthur Upshaw. The two sources on which he had been counting, both barren. Upshaw seemed to fear that if the brothers got together they would make common cause and flee with the booty; a suspicion undoubtedly reinforced by Darrell's refusal to show the letter.

Darrell rounded the hairpin bend, and a moment or so later passed back below the McKinstry villa. He looked up through heavy shrubbery overhanging the road, toward the back of the house. A single dim light showed, from an upstairs window.

Behind him appeared headlights; the Mercedes-Benz swerved to a stop. Ellen looked out at him with sullen hostility. "Jump in."

Darrell smiled and shook his head. "It's very decent of you —" here Ellen snorted "— but I prefer to walk. You English people live under such a strain, you drive yourselves and your cars at such a nerve-racking pace —"

"Oh dry up," muttered Ellen. "Are you getting in or not? And I'm not English, I'm Scottish."

"If you'll keep all four wheels on the ground. Perhaps you'd like me to drive."

"No, thanks. Please get in."

Darrell opened the door, gingerly settled himself. She started off with a roar, with a sly sidelong look at Darrell, but thereafter drove at a fairly conservative speed.

"Where do you want to go?"

"My hotel, I suppose. The Miranda."

There was a moment of awkward silence. Once or twice Ellen half started to speak. Finally she said, "By the way, if you're thinking of going to the police, I wouldn't."

"Ah!" said Darrell. "I understand now."

"You understand what?"

"Your altruism in coming after me. Uncle Arthur thought of something he'd neglected to tell me."

She drove several blocks in silence. "In any event, the police are not likely to be of any help."

"Why not? What are they paid for?"

"Use your brain. Noel is missing."

"That's what everybody tells me."

"Why are persons usually missing?"

"For various reasons."

"Reasons connected with loot. To be quite blunt, Noel has hopped the twig."

"I don't think so."

"Oh you don't?" Her voice trembled with scorn. "So Noel is virtuous and forbearing. Pious and good."

"Noel is a retarded adolescent, but not a thief."

Ellen laughed mockingly. "These windy assertions — what do they prove?" She swung the car to the curb in front of the Hotel Miranda. "Of course he's a crook! Why else did he duck out?"

"He might have run into trouble. An accident, perhaps."

"If there was an accident, he could have telephoned. No, he just saw a good thing and helped himself. But don't think the police can help you, because they can't. And wouldn't if they could."

"This is all far over my head. I can't quite believe that —"

Ellen made a furious gesture. "Very well, listen! I'll tell you what everybody knows anyway. Smuggling is a thing of the past around here. But there's money in gun-running."

"Gun-running? To whom? The Algerian rebels? The FLN, whatever they call it?"

"Yes, naturally. It's dangerous, because the French still maintain troops in Morocco. But if you're willing to take risks, it's worth your while."

"It seems rather a roundabout route to Algeria."

"Not at all. It's one of the most direct. Don't forget, the French patrol the Mediterranean. Every few months they stop a ship and seize the cargo. But with proper organization, other cargoes get through, and Uncle Arthur —" she spoke the name with a flat intonation "— bought such a cargo."

"Isn't this all rather casual? Presumably the French have agents in Tangier."

"The streets are thick with them. The operation naturally is supposed to be secret. Thanks to your precious Noel the whole town is laughing at Arthur."

"But how could Noel —"

Ellen interrupted impatiently. "The Algerians paid for the whole shipment, but they received less than a tenth of what they paid for. The manufacturer's agent won't release the balance of the weapons until he's paid. And Noel has the loot. So now you know why Noel is not exactly popular around Tangier."

"Yes," said Darrell. "It becomes clear."

"In any event you'll gain nothing from the police. They know the trade is going on. They're Moslems, they're sympathetic to the FLN. They don't care how many guns get through, the more the better. If you complain about Noel, you're talking about something they don't want to hear. You might even find yourself ejected as an undesirable."

Darrell opened the door, descended to the ground. Ellen watched him with raised eyebrows. She said in a pleasant voice, "If I were you, I'd clear out and leave Noel to stew in his own juice."

Darrell stood looking down at her. "That's a peculiar thing to say."

"Why peculiar?"

"I just arrived. You don't expect me to leave just like that."

"You might be wiser."

"I've been wise all my life. Noel's been foolish and he's had all the fun."

"He's not having fun now," said Ellen. "Wherever he is." She snatched at the gearbox; the engine growled; the convertible sprang down the street. Darrell watched it around the corner. He sighed, shook his head, went into the hotel.

The desk clerk handed him an envelope printed with his name. It contained a newspaper clipping. The headline read:

TORTURE VICTIM
FOUND IN FIELD

Darrell turned to the clerk. "Who brought this?"

"A boy."

"You don't know him?"

"No, sir."

Darrell read the clipping through:

TANGIER, March 28 — The mutilated body of Mohammed Ali Aktouf, 58, was found last night by a farm laborer in a field 20 kilometers south of Tangier, a few meters off the road connecting Sidi Boussen with the Tangier-Rabat highway. He was victim to one of the most sadistic assaults of recent years.

Aktouf's ankles and wrists were bound with copper wire. His body had been badly burnt, apparently with a petrol blowtorch. The cause of death is presumed to be heart failure, since Aktouf had a medical history of heart disease.

Officers of the Sûreté Nationale are investigating the crime but state that they have no clues as to either the identity of the torturers or their motive.

Aktouf, employed at a local hotel, a man of modest means, had no criminal record and was not known to be involved in political activity. There is speculation that the crime was a gruesome case of mistaken identity or possibly the work of Pan-Arab terrorists.

Aktouf's employer, Mr. Arthur Upshaw, Calle Miranda 37, has reported his accounts to be in good order, with no shortage of funds and no thefts reported at the hotel.

Darrell crossed the street to the Masquerade Bar.

CHAPTER V

THE MASQUERADE BAR was noisy and gay. The booths were crowded; two white-coated waiters ran back and forth. Phil Beresford, assisted by a second bartender, mixed drinks, chaffed the customers, rang the cash register, greeted newcomers, consoled the departing. Mr. Burdette emerged from the kitchen chewing and patting his mouth with plump little fingers; Phil feigned astonishment. Mr. Burdette gave a nonchalant wave of the hand, walked into the Balmoral lobby.

Darrell seated himself at the far end of the bar. Phil Beresford came to serve him. "I see you're back in one piece."

"Just barely. Can I get something to eat?"

"You certainly can. All we serve is food, nothing fancy. The steaks sometimes are pretty good." He squinted around the room. "I can't put you in a booth; do you want to eat right here?"

Darrell nodded. "A steak sounds fine, medium, and a bottle of beer."

"Right." Phil called the order into the kitchen, spread a napkin on the bar, set out a knife and fork. "How did you get along with Arthur Upshaw?"

"I don't know much more now than I did before. Except that Upshaw doesn't like to be fooled with."

"I could've told you that," said Phil. He poured a bottle of beer, went to serve another customer. Ten minutes later he brought the steak. "Ketchup? Worcestershire?"

"No, thanks. Take a look at this." He pushed the clipping across the bar.

Phil read, wrinkled his long nose in distaste. "A mess. I guess they never found out anything more. Poor old Aktouf. He worked right here in the Balmoral. I guess you knew that."

Darrell nodded, returned the clipping to the envelope. "It came tonight by messenger."

"Somebody thinks you need advice."

"It might even be considered a gentle hint."

"Could be."

Phil sprang down the bar to attend to the wants of a thirsty patron.

Presently he returned. "Everything okay?"

"Fine."

Phil looked over his shoulder down the bar. There was a lull; the other bartender was handling the business. Phil ducked under the counter, pulled over a stool. "Funny things happen in this town. I'm just a newcomer — I've been here eight years — but the tales I've heard…" He looked sidewise at Darrell. "What did Upshaw tell you?"

"Nothing very much. What he did tell me he labeled confidential."

"All these secrets." Phil drummed his fingers on the bar. "Upshaw is about to lose his shirt."

"That bad, eh?"

"Worse. His shirt and most of his underpants. He worked up this big deal, he sank every cent he could raise into it. He put the hotel up the spout, he got Duff to take a loan on the house, borrowed on the *Deirdre*. Instead of a bonanza, a fiasco. That's why I'm sweating. I got the most miserable lease in the world."

Darrell ordered a second bottle of beer. "How about you?"

"I never refuse."

The bartender brought Phil a highball. Phil cradled the glass in his fingers, considered the motion of the bubbles. "Upshaw is like one of the old-time maharajahs. When he dies the whole palace brigade throws themselves into the grave. When Upshaw goes, we all go — me, Ellen, Duff, the whole caboodle, wailing and screaming."

"Why Duff and Ellen? Don't they have a father and mother?"

"Dead." Phil swallowed two-thirds of the highball. "They're one of the old families, go back to the last century. Ben Upshaw, the grandfather, got run out of Scotland and came here. Arthur is his son." He finished the highball, looked reflectively at the ice. Darrell signaled the bartender.

"I never refuse," said Phil. "Well, to make a long story short, Peggy, Ben Upshaw's daughter and Arthur's sister, married Scotty McKinstry.

Arthur and Scotty worked together; they bought the first *Deirdre* and made good money. When Grandpa Upshaw died he left the house to Scotty and Peggy, this building here to Arthur. Times was good; Arthur put his money into the hotel. Scotty blew his on this and that. Peggy died, and just after I arrived Scotty stopped a Spanish bullet off Alicante. Duff and Ellen got the house, a little income, not much. Duff worked with Arthur on the new *Deirdre* and they did pretty good until things closed up. Then Arthur hatched this other big deal. Duff was all for it but Ellen, out of sheer cussedness, wouldn't let 'em mortgage the house until they gave her a down payment on that big black widow-maker she drives. I guess they hoped she'd kill herself." Phil ducked back under the bar, prepared to go to work. "Well, that's how the story goes. They had a sure thing, then something happened. And now they're all bollixed up."

There was a rustle of movement beside Darrell, a smell of violets, a swish of silky chestnut hair. "It's T-Bone the war correspondent," exclaimed Phil, "and her handsome young millionaire. Where have you been?"

"We've had dinner out at Cape Spartel," said T-Bone. "It was lovely! First lobster in coral sauce, and then some little partridges and then chateaubriand. Harvey ordered three bottles of champagne. Isn't he nice?" She patted the arm of her raw-boned young escort, who beamed proudly.

"You eat like that you'll ruin your lovely figure," said Phil.

"I eat every chance I get. I never know when will be my next meal."

Phil shook his head. "Never worry, T-Bone. Not while there's millionaires like Harvey to take starving young women under their wings."

"Harvey isn't a millionaire!"

"Right now ah'm just a private fust-class," said Harvey, "but ah'm from Texas, and they's still hope if ah scratch around a little. Ah'll make sahgeant too. Ain't you gonna bring us nothin' to drink?"

"Sure I'm going to bring you something to drink! That's my business. You call it, I bring it."

"I want a crème-de-menthe frappé," said T-Bone.

"Bonzo. Make that two, whatevah it is."

"With cherries, Phil."

Phil sighed, shook his head. "T-Bone, you're making an old man of me. When are you going back to Paris?"

"I don't know. I don't have any money."

"T-Bone's on the lam," Phil told Darrell. "She's committed a little peccadillo on the Champs-Elysées — debrained an old man with an axe, or something similar. They chased her to Rome, in and out of St. Tropez, but she ducked 'em at Majorca. She's waiting here till the indignation dies down."

"Phil! I never did any such thing!"

"Don't apologize, T-Bone. He was probably making a pest of himself."

Harvey descended from the stool, took T-Bone's drink. "C'mon honey-pup. I see a booth, let's join the humans."

T-Bone allowed herself to be led to a vacant booth. Phil and Darrell watched her cross the floor.

"Is she English?" Darrell asked. "She has some kind of accent."

"French and English. Her father's professor of archaeology at the Sorbonne, believe it or not. Contrary to rumor, it's T-Bone's father who pays her rent. Costs him half what he makes, no doubt."

"What is she doing here?"

"Heaven only knows. Maybe she just likes the place. T-Bone's a woman of mystery. She's also bird dog to a couple of newspapermen around town. Don't tell her anything you're ashamed of; you'll have your secrets all over the front pages."

"I can see how Noel would be interested."

Phil nodded. "She wouldn't play. Not very hard. T-Bone is highly moral. She wants holy wedlock. It's gotta wear pants, carry a big bankroll, and use an American passport. She hasn't had much luck around here. The Americans have all been raggedy-ass fugitives like me and Harvey; the rich blokes have big bellies and wives. Duff's the one who's got it bad. If he comes in, look for trouble."

"What kind of trouble?"

"He kinda drew a line around T-Bone." Phil shook his head ruefully. "One time I had to give him a real serious talking to. I said, 'Duff, you swing on me, you'll be minus a bowel. I don't like this brawling. I'm delicate.'" A customer signaled and Phil moved off down the bar.

Darrell sat drinking his beer and musing. Ideas passed through his mind like pedestrians hurrying through the rain — images, half-formed speculations, fleeting tail ends of recollections: the fact of Noel's disappearance, the letter which occasioned so much interest…Blank-eyed Arthur Upshaw, truculent Duff McKinstry. Ellen…The clipping describing the death of Mohammed Ali Aktouf, the desk clerk at the Balmoral Hotel…Mrs. Ritterman, with the hair hanging down her face like seaweed over a rock…Noel's pathetic excuse for a boat…Across the room in a booth, T-Bone…

Phil Beresford's voice came from close beside his shoulder. "Watching T-Bone gets to be a kind of disease. I'm saving my cigarette money; as soon as I get a million, I'm gonna propose."

"I thought you were married."

Phil made an airy gesture. "The work of a minute. This is a Moslem country. All I gotta do is say 'I renounce thee' three times and bingo! That's it. I already said it twice." Phil's gaze focused on the door. He clapped his hand to the side of his head. "Oh oh. Here it comes."

Duff stalked in, swung up on a bar stool, turned a brief cool stare at Darrell.

"Hello, Duff," said Phil heartily. "Where you been this time of night?"

"Down on the boat. Weeds a yard long, deck going to hell."

"Put on fiberglass, like I told you. You'll get a better price."

"Over the teak? Good lord! You Yanks are barbarians." He seemed to see T-Bone for the first time, and groaned. "Where did she locate that specimen? What is it?"

"A resident of the great state of Texas, now employed by the United States Army."

"That's the absolute limit." Duff winced.

"It seems reasonable to me," said Phil. "She got hungry and Harvey fed her. I don't think the attraction goes much further. Although Harvey plans to be a millionaire."

Duff swung around with a sardonic twist to his mouth. "She told me she was staying in. Little dickens."

"A hungry woman don't stay in, that's well known." Phil moved off to attend to a customer. Duff looked into the mirror behind the bar, then turned to Darrell. "So now what'll you do?"

"I don't know. According to Mr. Upshaw you and he already went to look for Noel."

"We did that."

"And you found nothing? No leads? Nothing?"

"Nothing."

"Where did you go to look?"

Duff laughed. "A professional secret, old boy."

"I'm not in the profession. Why not cooperate?"

"Don't care for any, thank you. Do your own dirty work."

"But if there's any chance —"

"There isn't. Noel has taken to the tall grass. My guess is Casablanca." He looked over his shoulder. Harvey was holding T-Bone's fingers in his big red fists. Duff snorted in disgust. He stepped down off the stool, walked across the bar.

"Here it comes," groaned Phil. "Some day, some day…"

Duff bent over T-Bone, remonstrating. Harvey stared at Duff, morosely attacked his green drink. T-Bone smiled, made her prettiest excuses. Duff argued. Harvey slowly raised his head, squinting up at Duff. He spoke with cold Texas formality. Duff made a cool retort, turned his shoulder. Harvey brooded for a few seconds, his face red. He put his hands on the table. He spoke: an ultimatum. Duff glanced at him disdainfully. Harvey hoisted himself to his feet.

With a rapidity almost magic Phil stood beside the booth. "First settle the bill, then outside."

Harvey tossed a pair of dollar bills on the table. He and Duff marched to the door, followed by a string of curiosity seekers.

Phil returned behind the bar. "Every week, once a week, it happens."

"Duff doesn't show any scars," observed Darrell.

"He's pretty good by now. He's quick and mean; he don't get excited."

T-Bone flounced across the room, stood fuming beside the bar. "That Duff! I wish he'd leave me alone!"

"Don't encourage him."

"But I don't!"

"Sure you do. You can't help it."

"I'm never, never, never going to talk to him again."

From outside came sounds of conflict: cries, blows, curses. Phil listened with a critical ear. "Harvey seems to be holding his own."

"I wish he'd *kill* Duff."

"No such luck."

There were whistles, sharp commands, a sudden cessation of movement, then measured official voices. "The gendarmes," said Phil. "A short walk up from the corner."

"I'm going to bed," said T-Bone. She walked swiftly through the connecting door into the lobby of the Balmoral. Customers filed back into the bar. Duff marched in, arms swinging wide, eyes glowing. Harvey followed, slouching angrily. He was disheveled; his cheek was bruised; he looked as if he had fallen. He searched around the room. "Where'd she go?" he asked in a thick voice.

"She said to thank you for a pleasant evening," said Phil, "and ran off to bed."

Harvey hesitated, looked at Duff, who leaned against the bar. Harvey slowly turned away, evidently aching to demolish the entire interior, then walked with slow steps to the door. Here he turned a last look toward Duff, who made no move. Harvey departed.

Duff rubbed his knuckles. "Nothing like a little sport to liven a dull evening." He turned a level glance toward Darrell, who made no comment.

Five minutes later Arthur Upshaw strode smartly in from the Balmoral lobby. At the sight of Darrell he stopped short, then came over to the bar. "I still hope to see that letter, Mr. Hutson."

"That's a forlorn hope, Mr. Upshaw."

"We may still come to an understanding." He nodded to Phil. "Plain whiskey and soda." Signaling to Duff he crossed the room, settled into the booth vacated by Harvey and T-Bone. Duff joined him; they conversed earnestly.

Darrell paid his bill. He pushed through the door, stepped out on the sidewalk. The time was eleven o'clock, Calle Miranda was quiet. Street lamps shone through the acacia trees; century plants made a jungle of sharp wild shadows behind him; cars crouched in the gutter like the hulks of dead beetles.

A figure left the dark blot of a doorway, stood waiting. Green light from the MASQUERADE sign shone on his face: Slip-Slip the Moroccan.

"Good night, Mr. Hutson," he called softly. "Good night, how are you?"

"I'm well. How are you?"

"Good." The hazel eyes glittered in the green light. "You looking for your brother Noel?"

"Yes."

"You want to find him?"

"Yes. Do you know where he is?"

"Maybe I know a man who knows where is Mr. Noel. You want to come see?"

"Tonight? No."

"No, not tonight. Maybe tomorrow. First I find out. But you come, eh?"

"That all depends."

"Sure. I know. Maybe I see you tomorrow. Then you go talk to the man. Good, eh?"

"Good, maybe. Where is this man?"

"That's what is maybe. Tonight what you do?"

"I go to bed."

"You want something?"

"No, thanks."

"You like to look at some girls? Maybe just look, maybe you like."

"No, I don't think so."

"You like anything else?"

"No. Just bed."

Darrell started away, looked back. Slip-Slip stood watching him, lonesome and wistful.

Darrell went up to his room. From his suitcase he took the letter Noel had written home. He looked at it a moment, weighed it in his hand. He left the room, returned downstairs. At the desk he requested an envelope, bought a stamp. He addressed the envelope to himself, care of American Express, Tangier. He tucked Noel's letter within, dropped it into the mailbox. Then he climbed the steps to his room, locked the door, went to bed.

Chapter VI

Darrell sat at a sidewalk café looking across the Place de France. The population of Tangier passed in front of him: ragged Berbers, sleek Spaniards, tourists of every description. There were men in fez and djellaba with European shoes; men in slacks and sport coat with fez and white Moroccan slippers. There were women in tweed suits, women in California sportswear, women veiled to the eyes with white robes sweeping the sidewalk. Vendors of silk scarfs, bright-colored skull-caps, toy balloons, jewelry, gewgaws and oddments prowled the sidewalk eyeing the café customers. The sun shone brightly, the air was heavy with the scent of acacia. Darrell sipped mint tea from a thick glass, considered his visit to the American consulate.

The interview had been unrewarding — predictably so, Darrell recognized. He had been received with promptness, heard with courtesy. He had detailed as many circumstances as he thought necessary; the consul had been sympathetic but uncooperative. "You have consulted the police? I presume not, since your brother was involved in illegal activity."

"It's been suggested," said Darrell, "that the police look the other way in these matters."

The consul shrugged. "I can't make any official comment as to that. However, times being as they are…Cigarette?"

"No, thanks."

The consul leaned back in his chair, looked reflectively out the window. "It's a difficult situation for you."

"Yes," said Darrell. "I feel rather helpless. Unofficially, what do you think happened to him?"

"A month ago he left Tangier with a load of guns and hasn't been heard from? My guess is that he's dead. The French take a dim view of gun-running. In the second place, other groups — rival groups, you might say — work out of both Tangier and Casablanca. Violence, hijacking, murder — they've all occurred in the past. Perhaps you read of the launches which were blown up in the harbor? No? There was considerable publicity."

He put his hands briskly on the table; the interview was over. Darrell stood up. "Thank you for your time, at least."

"Not at all. I can only make the obvious suggestion: go to the police. If and when they locate him, if and when they place him under arrest, I'll see that he has the help he's entitled to."

Darrell sipped the mint tea. He had expected no more from the consul, but it was a step he felt bound to take. An urchin approached, took a large rubber tarantula from a basket, set it on the table. The legs moved, the thing gave a jump. "How much, mister? How much you give?"

"No, thank you. I'm not interested."

"Very cheap. Look." The rubber insect leapt forward.

"I don't want it."

"How much? Six hundred francs? That's a good price."

"No, thanks."

"Look at this." He produced a rubber figure which, on manipulation of a pneumatic bulb, kicked out its legs and arms. "You like better? I give you a good price."

"I don't care for either one of the things."

"Both for eight hundred francs. Very good. You won't get no cheaper anywhere. You look, you try. This is cheap price."

"I'm not in the market."

"How much you give? How much?"

"Nothing."

"I give to you for seven hundred."

"No."

"Just today, six hundred."

"No."

"Okay, mister, okay. Don't get sore." He departed to place his tarantula in front of two elderly ladies eating ice cream. Darrell continued his contemplation. So far as he could determine, he had reached a dead end. Slip-Slip had offered mysterious hints, which probably would come to nothing except requests for money. Still they supplied a pretext for further consultation with Arthur Upshaw, during which he might glean one or two fragments of information. He had nothing better to do, in any event. He paid the waiter, rose from his table, walked up the hill to the Hotel Balmoral.

Arthur Upshaw was not in. The desk clerk professed ignorance as to where he could be found.

Darrell returned to the street. He hailed a cab, gave the address of the McKinstry house on Calle Costanza.

Arriving, he found the Mercedes-Benz parked in the driveway. When he rang the bell, Ellen opened the door. Standing with the shadows of the house behind her, wearing threadbare blue jeans and a dark blue cotton T-shirt, she had for a moment the look of dreaming adolescence. She stared at Darrell from dispassionate gray eyes. "Hello. What do you want?"

"I'd like to talk to your uncle, if he's available at the moment."

"He's not here."

"Do you expect him?"

"No. This isn't his home. I don't invite him; he merely comes." Her voice had taken on a faint ring, like a cymbal brushed with a coat sleeve.

"Do you know where I can find him?"

Ellen eyed him with suspicion. "Why all the urgency?"

"I hope I can persuade him Noel isn't as guilty as he thinks."

Ellen laughed grimly. "You'll find that Arthur is immune to your charm, Mr. Hutson."

"I wasn't aware that you'd noticed it."

Ellen swept him with an icy glance.

"Excuse me," said Darrell.

"Come along," she muttered ungraciously, "I'll take you to Arthur."

"That's not necessary," said Darrell. "Just tell me where he is; I've got a cab waiting."

"I'm not sure myself. I've nothing better to do anyway."

She jumped down from the porch, into the Mercedes-Benz with an artless disregard for dignity that Darrell suddenly found ingratiating. No matter how provoking her arrogance it was hard to dislike her.

He paid off his cab, seated himself beside her. With a roar and gnash of tires they were away. Trees and houses flashed past; they tracked along the road like a bobsled down a run. Darrell put his hand on the ignition key. "Must you drive so fast?"

Ellen darted him a malicious glance, reduced her speed. At a relatively moderate pace they reached the main part of town, crossed the Boulevard Pasteur, swung on down the hill. At a dingy yellow stucco building Ellen stopped the car, jumped to the sidewalk. The door bore letters in flaking gold leaf which read:

OSCAR VENTRISS

General Agent

Ellen opened the door, walked inside; after a moment's hesitation Darrell followed.

A fat man in a brown suit and a broad-brimmed brown homburg looked up. He took the cigar from his wet pink mouth. "Well?"

"Is Mr. Upshaw here?"

Ventriss shook his head, replaced the cigar in his mouth, stared from small black eyes. "He comes, he goes."

"Where did he go?"

Ventriss popped his eyes, waved a fat pink hand. "How would I know?" He jerked his thumb at Darrell. "Who is this gentleman?"

"This is Noel Hutson's brother."

Ventriss chuckled — a doleful gurgle, like a bilge pump sucking air. "You are sure?"

"I really don't care, one way or the other."

Ventriss shook his head in disapproval. "Now they come. From all directions. Like flies." He turned back to his desk, sliding the cigar to the other side of his mouth.

Ellen motioned to Darrell. "Let's go."

They returned to the car. "Now where?" asked Darrell.

"There's another place he might be." She turned up the hill.

Darrell asked, "Does Ventriss have something to do with Noel?"

"Not directly."

"General Agent — he represents the weapons manufacturer. Am I right?"

"What difference does it make?" Ellen asked in utter boredom. "Unless you plan to place an order of your own. It's cash on the nail. No credit."

"He's the man to see? The importer, so to speak?"

She turned an appraising glance at him. "You're very interested, aren't you?"

"No. Not really. As you say, what difference does it make?"

The conversation languished. Back up the hill they drove, bearing westward toward the ancient fortress — the kasbah which dominated the medina. Darrell asked politely, "Where are we going now?"

"Tracking down Arthur. It's certain that Ventriss refused to release any more merchandise without payment, so Arthur will automatically try to squeeze the other end of the business."

"The FLN?"

"Call it that if you like."

"What do you call it?"

"Egypt. UAR. Pan-Arabia. The Moslem Empire. FLN is only a front — the people that do the fighting. In another ten years…well, there may still be a few Europeans alive in North Africa."

The street opened into an enormous square, clotted with the stalls of flower vendors. At the far end rose the minaret of a mosque.

Ellen parked the Mercedes-Benz. "Come along."

"Where are we going?"

"Down to Soco Chico."

"Who may that be?"

She gave him a glance of contemptuous amusement. "This square is the Soco Grande. Soco Chico is another square further down. It's easier to walk than to drive."

She led the way into a street lined with money changers' booths, and the shops of Indian merchants. The crowd was almost wholly Moroccan, the men wearing fezzes, turbans, multicolored skull-caps; the women nondescript behind veils. Minute donkeys overloaded with hides, vegetables, fodder, staggered down the middle of the street.

Two or three hundred yards from Soco Grande they broke into Soco Chico, narrow and shadowed under five-story buildings with decaying woodwork and weathered brown paint. "You wait here," said Ellen. "I'll be gone only a minute."

Darrell watched the slender, rather taut figure in blue jeans disappear into a side street. The minute stretched into two; Darrell stepped over to a nearby café, took a seat at a sidewalk table and watched the passers-by. A waiter approached; Darrell ordered a bottle of beer.

Five minutes later Ellen returned, coming across the dingy picturesque little square, threading through the Moroccans with a jaunty elastic stride. Her gaze was focused on nothing, her expression was something between indifference and disdain. It came to Darrell with a faint sense of surprise that Ellen was a pretty girl. Her tawny hair was clean and fine; she had admirable clear eyes, square shoulders and slim hips — the figure of a tennis player. She felt Darrell's gaze; her mouth took on a sardonic twist. "They've gone. I can't find anyone."

"Sit down," said Darrell. "Have a drink."

She looked at him quizzically. "A social invitation?"

"Yes, I suppose that's what it amounts to."

Ellen compressed her mouth until the lips were almost invisible and little creases, like smile marks, appeared at the corners. "Perhaps you'll tell me why you wanted to see Arthur?"

"If you'll tell me one or two things in return."

"Maybe." She lowered herself into a chair. The waiter approached. Ellen spoke three words in Arabic; the waiter bowed, retreated. Ellen looked sidewise at Darrell with curiosity and calculation. "Well? Why all the rush to find Arthur?"

"To tell the complete truth," said Darrell, "I had to do something, and talking to Mr. Upshaw was as good as anything."

Ellen nodded, mouth twisted more sardonically than ever. "And I drive you all over town merely because you feel restless."

"Not quite. A couple things have happened."

The waiter returned with a small cup of black coffee, set it before Ellen.

"I hoped," said Darrell, "that I could trade information with Mr. Upshaw."

"Hmf. That's a useless hope. What's happened?"

"I've been approached by a Moroccan, who said he could give me information. That was last night. I didn't see him this morning, but no doubt he'll show up. I suppose money will change hands."

"You'll be sold a pup."

Darrell shrugged. "Perhaps. There's a chance —"

"No chance whatever. If anyone wanted to sell information they'd have gone to Arthur long ago."

"True. Unless —"

"Unless what?"

"Nothing really. There are a hundred possibilities. Suppose the Moroccan came direct from Noel?"

She laughed. "Much more likely that our friend Noel saw a good thing, and took it."

Darrell shook his head. "I know Noel too well."

"He'd turn down four hundred thousand pounds? Over a million dollars?"

Darrell looked off across the square. "The figure has a certain glamour... The glamour might tempt Noel... but I still don't believe it. The whole thing is ridiculous. Who'd be fool enough to hand that much money over to him?"

"Who said anything about money?"

Darrell raised his eyebrows. "You did. Four hundred thousand pounds."

"Four hundred thousand pounds' worth of heroin."

Something inside Darrell took a queer lurch, the skin of his face contracted. He sat back in his chair and contemplated Ellen with fascination. She watched him with a cool half-grin. Darrell's convictions regarding Noel returned with greater intensity than ever. He felt excited and feverish, and the awareness of his emotion made him angrier than ever. "Beyond any possible doubt, you're wrong," he finally said. "It's just possible that Noel might steal a million dollars. But he'd never touch a dime's worth of heroin."

"It's gone and Noel's gone with it." Ellen was grinning openly. "Why are you so upset?"

"I had no idea you were in the dope business." Darrell was surprised to hear himself say this. Ellen seemed surprised too. The grin faded, her face became cold.

"I'm not — if it makes any difference. Arthur and Duff aren't either. They buy and sell commodities and arrange for their transportation. They serve a function, they don't make judgments."

"That's pretty glib. Do you tell yourself that often?"

"I never think of it. As a matter of fact, I don't work with Duff and Arthur. I detest Arthur and quarrel with Duff."

"You have an odd set of moral principles."

Ellen sat back, stretched out her fine slim legs. "I don't have any moral principles — except the principle of self-interest. Precisely like everyone else, though other people profess noble ideals. I profess to nothing."

"Do you enjoy injuring other people?"

"Not at all. I'm free from sadism, masochism and any other ism — or so I believe."

"Still, you must know what dope addiction does to people."

"Certainly. Almost as much damage as cigarette smoking." She raised herself energetically in her seat. "Don't preach to me about narcotic rings. Nobody passes any laws about the tobacco industry. Compared with them, narcotics peddling is kid stuff."

"You make a very convincing point; in fact, you press it rather heatedly —"

"Not at all; I merely want to drive it home."

"In which case, why don't you show the same indignation about narcotics?"

"My dear young man, I'm not at all indignant. I merely observe that many socially accepted enterprises profit from potential harm done to their fellow men. The presidents of the tobacco companies aren't indicted for murder. So when you sit here wringing your hands over the narcotic traffic, I merely wonder whether you are a hypocrite or a fool, or something of both."

Darrell grimly set about the task of collecting his wits. "Have you come to any decision?"

"It's not important."

"You feel then that because some people are scoundrels, you can be a scoundrel too."

"I really don't care," said Ellen flippantly. "Haven't I told you I have no moral sense? None whatever. I observe the minimum number of social conventions, and if I'm neither a cigarette nor a narcotic salesman it's for no reasons of morality. But I'm running low on funds and soon I'll have to turn my hand to something. There is only one logical move."

"Rather an untidy business."

"Not if the price is right."

"How much do you plan to charge?"

She looked at him sidelong. "Oh — a hundred, perhaps. As much as the traffic will bear."

Darrell counted out some change. "There's a hundred and fifty."

She looked at it with raised eyebrows. "In francs? That's hardly flattering. I was thinking in terms of pounds."

"A hundred pounds. That's rather high."

"Not so high. I'll make it interesting."

"No doubt. How about fifty?"

"Let's see your money. Or is this just talk?"

"Just talk. Fifty pounds is a hundred and forty dollars."

Ellen got to her feet. "If we don't find Noel fairly soon, I'll cut prices. Are you coming?"

"Wait. I'd like to show you something."

She sat down again. "What?"

Darrell gave her the clipping he had received. "What do you make of this?"

She read the clipping, returned it. "What about it?"

"It came in an envelope addressed to me."

"If I were you, I'd go home."

"That seems to be the message. Does your immorality extend to torture?"

She darted him a swift glance. "No. Not through lack of immorality. Lack of nerve and enterprise. Hmm. It never occurred to me that Aktouf might know anything. I can't imagine why anyone should think he did."

"I don't suppose, then, that you sent me this clipping?"

She shook her head. "As I've told you I have no personal concern with this business."

"I thought your money was tied up in it."

"Like a fool I let Duff mortgage the house and realize our capital. Unless Noel shows up it's gone. I'll lose the car; Duff will owe me twenty thousand pounds which of course I'll never see. To that extent I'm anxious to see Noel."

Darrell crumpled the clipping, tossed it into the gutter. "It's a good guess that Aktouf was tortured for information."

"If you're wondering who did it," said Ellen coldly, "the answer is, I don't know. I did not. Duff could not do it alone; he has no real will of his own. Arthur is capable of any cruelty. I owe my present clear-sighted outlook on life to Arthur." She jumped to her feet, turned her head away with a jerk that sent her blonde-brown hair flying. "Let's go," she said in a muffled voice.

Chapter VII

Darrell lunched in a quiet restaurant off the Place de France. Ellen had sneered at his suggestion that she join him, had jumped in her car and roared off across the Soco Grande scattering pedestrians like chickens.

As he ate he pondered Ellen. Pretty girls were seldom misanthropes. The usual run of anti-social rebels — the anarchists, existentialists, bop mystics, beatniks, Trotskyites, nihilists, pacifists, outsiders, angry young men, Platonic aristocrats — huddled in careful cliques, fearing nothing more than the absence of social order. Ellen walked alone. She admitted to at least indirect involvement in the narcotics trade; she had offered herself for fifty pounds, she had jeered when he balked at the price. She drove like a madwoman, contemptuous of life and limb. She proudly claimed immorality for a creed. Misfit, thought Darrell, was something of an understatement. The word depravity came to mind but it failed to ring true. Ellen looked anything but depraved; depravity was moral collapse. Ellen was too stubborn and bitter and intelligent for collapse. Peculiar, thought Darrell.

As an exercise in incongruity he transposed Ellen to his home environment; he pictured her shopping in a supermarket, sunning herself beside the back-yard swimming pool, pelting along the freeway in her Mercedes-Benz. And strangely the pictures weren't grotesque at all; Ellen looked bright and happy. Darrell roused himself.

He paid his check, left the restaurant in a mood of depression. He walked to the telephone office, put a call through to the United States, reached his father without difficulty. He reported what he had learned, added one or two of his speculations.

"Apparently Noel's been traveling with a rough crowd," came his father's voice.

"Yes, it looks that way."

"Well, don't take any risks. I don't want you in trouble on Noel's account."

"We're agreed there. Well, I'll keep plugging. Maybe something will turn up. I'll call back in a day or two."

"Right. Take care of yourself."

"I'll be careful. Good-by."

"Good-by."

Darrell walked down the hill to Calle Erasmus and the Hotel de los Dos Continentes. He found Mrs. Ritterman on her knees scrubbing the front steps. At the sight of Darrell, she raised up on her knees, wiped her nose with her forearm. "Now what is it?"

Darrell said politely, "I suppose you've had no news of Noel."

Mrs. Ritterman said suspiciously, "I think something wrong goes on. You are his brother?"

"Yes, of course I'm his brother."

"That is what you say."

Darrell brought out his passport. "Check on this. Here's my name: Darrell Hutson."

Mrs. Ritterman hauled herself to her feet with a grunt. "It is very strange. A boy comes this morning who wants Noel's letters. He says Noel has told him to come."

"Did you give them to him?"

Mrs. Ritterman laughed indignantly. "You think I don't know my business? I tell him, bring a letter from Noel, that he wants to give these things to you. And he says yes, he will get the letter."

"How long ago was this?"

"This morning."

"And he said he was coming back today?"

"Yes. Look!" She took his elbow in one of her hands, pointed with the other. "It is him! That one!"

Darrell turned, observed Slip-Slip coming along the street. At the sight of Darrell, Slip-Slip halted, then came forward with a pleased smile. "Hello, Mr. Hutson. I'm glad to see you."

"I imagine you are. What do you want with Noel's letters?"

"Letters, Mr. Hutson?"

Darrell reached, took the paper the youth carried. He unfolded it. Careful round handwriting read:

> *Manager,*
> *Hotel de los Dos Continentes:*
> *Please give Suliman my post.*
> Mr. Noel Hutson

Darrell handed the letter to Mrs. Ritterman. She read without amusement, turned with her arm raised. Slip-Slip ducked back. "You think I am stupid? You think I get in trouble for nothing? Wait. I call the police."

Slip-Slip sidled away. "I was bringing the letters to you, Mr. Hutson. I think you want them."

"Thanks," said Darrell dryly.

"You want to know about your brother?"

"Naturally."

"I been trying to find out. Maybe tomorrow I come see you." He departed, looking back over his shoulder.

"That one is no good," declared Mrs. Ritterman. She pulled at her skirt preparing to resume work.

Darrell smoothed his voice into the accents of persuasion. "Would you let me see the letters?"

Mrs. Ritterman's face became determined; Darrell saw that he had been tactless. "No. I keep them. When Noel comes, I give him his post. No one else."

Argument was useless; Mrs. Ritterman was clearly an obstinate woman. Darrell asked politely, "Will you put the letters away, lock them up somewhere to keep them safe?"

"I lock them up. No one gets them."

Darrell walked to the Masquerade Bar, which at four-thirty was almost deserted. Phil Beresford stood writing in a canvas-bound ledger, heavy horn-rimmed glasses on his nose. T-Bone sat in front of him wearing a short-sleeved black frock, drinking a Tom Collins in which floated a dozen maraschino cherries.

"Good afternoon," said Phil. "I'm trying to balance my books, but T-Bone keeps breathing on me and frosting my glasses."

"You asked me to sit here," said T-Bone.

"You promised to behave. That means no breathing." He snapped shut the ledger. "I can't make these books balance and the reason is simple." He looked owlishly at Darrell. "I spend twice as much as I earn. What'll you have, Mr. Hutson?"

Darrell ordered a martini. T-Bone looked at him with knitted brows. "Noel's name was Hutson, too," she told Phil in wonder.

"That's how the system works," said Phil. "Brothers use the same last names."

"But I didn't know he was Noel's brother. Is he? Really?"

"Certainly he is. Doesn't he look like Noel?"

T-Bone laughed in sudden gayety. "Is he the one who makes so much money building highways?"

"Here we go," groaned Phil.

T-Bone turned so that she sat facing Darrell. She fished one of the cherries from the glass, nibbled at it. "You are older than Noel?"

"Two years."

"And you are not married?"

"I saw him first," said Phil. "Lay off."

T-Bone laughed in quiet superiority. "You're already married."

"I'm not planning bigamy," Phil explained. "I merely want to sell him a bar."

"Lord no," said Darrell.

"A fine going concern. Elite clientele, good stock, Arthur Upshaw for a landlord. Name a figure, any figure." He snapped his fingers. "I'll sell like that. Just so it's enough to get me and Flounce here to Honolulu. T-Bone, I tell you, it's wonderful. I got a little shack on the Kailua beach; what with you, me and the badger game, we'll do all right. The finest of fish, home brew, okulehao —"

"Sh," said T-Bone. "Mrs. Phil."

"So what? She knows, she's just waiting." But he looked over his shoulder. He turned back. "You little devil, trying to scare me like that."

"No, here she comes," said T-Bone.

Mrs. Phil came walking with her long slow strut from the kitchen. "You're wanted on the phone," she said gruffly. "It's Grandin, about the invoice."

"Okay, Mama, I'll take it here. 'Scuse me, folks." He ducked under the bar, crossed to the phone booth. Mrs. Phil, with the merest flicker of a glance toward T-Bone, strode back to the kitchen.

"Brrr," said T-Bone, pretending to shiver. "Like an ice cube." She glanced archly sidewise at Darrell. "Why are you looking at me like that?"

"I was wondering."

"About me?"

"Noel sent home a photograph of you and him on a beach."

T-Bone nodded without enthusiasm. She turned away from Darrell, as if the subject bored her.

Phil returned. "I'm gonna get that phone moved out of the kitchen for sure. It scares the customers to have Mama come sneaking in like that, and it scares me."

"She wants to see what's going on," said T-Bone sagely.

"She just likes to parade back and forth," said Phil. "When Mr. Burdette bit at her hook, she got to thinking of herself as a goddess."

T-Bone wrinkled her nose, and ate a cherry.

The glass and iron door from the Balmoral swung open; Arthur Upshaw and Duff came in. Upshaw signaled to Phil; they went to the far end of the bar and conferred earnestly. Duff planted himself beside T-Bone, with a scowling side-glance for Darrell. "Are you ready?"

"Yes," sighed T-Bone. "Where are we going?"

"To Graham's house for a drink."

T-Bone rubbed the tip of her finger in a spot of water on the bar, traced a wet circle.

"You act like you don't want to go," suggested Duff.

"I don't like Graham. He tells dirty jokes."

"We don't need to stay long."

T-Bone slid off the stool. "I've got such a headache, Duff. Really, I can't go anywhere."

"But I've already —"

"Good night, Duff." She turned a wistful smile toward Darrell. "Good night, Mr. Hutson."

"Good night."

T-Bone departed. As she passed into the lobby of the Balmoral, her pace quickened and she ran up the stairs.

Duff swung on his heel and left the bar.

Darrell sat watching Arthur Upshaw and Phil. Upshaw spoke forcefully; he slapped the bar with the tips of his fingers. Phil's face was long and doleful. He argued, protested.

Upshaw made a terse remark, turned away. He strode along the bar to Darrell. "Come over here, Mr. Hutson, if you will. I want to talk to you."

He motioned Darrell into a booth, sat down opposite. "You've been talking to my niece."

"Yes."

"I suppose that she's told you a great deal."

"Just the background of this business."

Upshaw bared his teeth in a swift grimace, fast as the flick of a camera shutter. "She'd do anything to spite me. Do you realize that this whole mess could have been avoided? If she had only come to me when Noel telephoned her."

"Noel telephoned her?"

Upshaw looked at Darrell sharply. "She did not mention this telephone call to you?"

"No."

"What did she tell you?"

"Enough that I understand what's going on."

Upshaw grunted. "I hardly need tell you that I don't want this information shared with French intelligence agents."

"I don't know any French intelligence agents."

"You've just been talking to one."

"Who? Phil?"

"No."

"You don't mean T-Bone?"

Upshaw held up his hand. "She's no undercover agent, but she has friends who are. They explain what they want to know, suggest persons to ask, and pay her if she's successful. I tell you this so that you'll be on your guard."

"But Duff—"

"Exactly. Why else do you think she tolerates him? I've explained this to Duff. His vanity resists the idea; nevertheless, he takes care to hold his tongue."

"Hmm."

"I also urge you not to confide in Beresford. He's careless, he drinks heavily and talks too much. If you make a call from the telephone booth, either he or his wife listens on the kitchen extension. They know more about my business than I do."

Darrell said nothing. Upshaw watched him with impassive eyes.

"There is considerable money at stake in this matter, as you now realize. One man, my former desk clerk, has already died—a futile death, since I'm sure he knew nothing. It might happen again. I suggest that you go home, and leave your brother to fend for himself."

"You hardly expect me to do that, Mr. Upshaw."

Upshaw said in a heavy voice of absolute conviction: "Noel has stolen a valuable consignment. So much is fact. At the worst he'll get only what he deserves."

Darrell restrained his first retort and said simply, "Noel wouldn't touch dope. He just wouldn't do it."

"The fact remains that he did do it. Otherwise, where is he? The French don't have him, nor the Moroccans. There's no one else. He's run off. Decamped."

"An accident—"

"We'd have found the truck. Don't forget, Mr. Hutson, a million dollars can sweeten a man's revulsion for most anything. In this regard, you personally are in a precarious position."

"That's ridiculous. I—"

Upshaw ignored the interruption. "Your brother disappears with a million dollars, is presumably waiting his chance to win free. At this juncture you appear. Personally I believe that you know nothing of Noel's whereabouts, but there are others who don't. I advise you to give me this ridiculous letter and get on home."

"I'll show you the letter—when you tell me what I want to know.

Where to look for Noel, what kind of truck he was driving, who he was supposed to meet, who he actually did meet, who knew where and when he was going."

Upshaw swung away without a word. Darrell returned to his seat at the bar, ordered another martini.

Phil served him, his silver-blond hair ruffled, his tie askew. He turned a waspish glance toward Upshaw. "You know this pecking order the chickens work up, where they all got someone lower than themselves they can peck? Well, I'm that poor wild bird at the bottom of the list. They all come flying when they get irritated. Arthur just now says he's raising the rent."

"Raising the rent? I thought he was losing the building."

"He's been haggling with the bank, trying to work something out. In the meantime he's broke and wants me to pay his way. He drives a big Chrysler, Ellen runs that insane black mowing machine. Me, I got a beat-up MG and Arthur thinks I should economize. It's a funny family, I'll tell you that much." He shot a lowering glance across the room.

"Tell me something," said Darrell. "Why does Ellen go around with a chip on her shoulder?"

"Search me. She's been queer ever since Scotty McKinstry got his off Alicante. That was eight years ago, when I first came here. She was a real pretty kid with big eyes and long hair; one of them Alice-in-Wonderland types. They sent her all over to school: England, Switzerland, France. She'd get kicked out just as fast as they enrolled her."

Customers entered; Phil became busy. Mr. Burdette came in with a chesty young matron who spoke in a hoarse growling voice. Arthur Upshaw ordered and ate dinner, interrupted once by Mrs. Phil, who summoned him to the telephone. Then he strode into the Balmoral lobby, looking neither right nor left.

Darrell presently left the Masquerade. He strolled the length of Boulevard Pasteur, dined in a cafeteria, bought a magazine and returned up Calle Miranda. He went up to his room, read for an hour, then tossed away the magazine and lay staring up at the ceiling. Light from the crackling green MASQUERADE shone through the window, enticing him almost against his will.

He went back downstairs, crossed the street, took his usual place at the bar. A few minutes later T-Bone peered cautiously in from the lobby of the Balmoral. Phil beckoned to her. "T-Bone! I thought you was in bed. Where you been?"

T-Bone sauntered over to the bar. "I'm going to bed now. A nice Swedish man telephoned, a Mr. Sverdlup. Do you know him?"

"Can't say as I have that honor."

"He took me to dinner, and I'm so tired. Good evening, Mr. Hutson."

"Good evening."

"Better not let your boy friend catch you out of your pajamas," said Phil. "His feelings might be hurt."

"Oh, that Duff!" T-Bone compressed her sweet mouth. "He's the worst nuisance. Absolutely impossible."

"That's the hazard of your profession."

"My profession?"

"Your main profession. Being beautiful for a living. We're all in love with you. Duff, me, Mr. Burdette, Mr. Hutson, everybody. All of us snapping and snarling and warning each other off."

T-Bone looked pertly at Darrell. "Mr. Hutson isn't in love with me. Are you, Mr. Hutson?"

Phil laughed gleefully. "What can he say? If he says no, he's a liar; if he says yes, he's got to feed you."

T-Bone said with quiet dignity, "He can take me to dinner even if he doesn't love me."

Phil clapped his hand to his forehead. "When will I learn? T-Bone, please don't marry Darrell. He's a civil engineer. He roams the wilderness, with no champagne for miles around. He eats hard-boiled eggs and soda crackers. He sleeps in a tent, usually with a big grizzly bear just outside. His blankets are all too short, and icicles hang from his toes. Right, Darrell?"

"More or less."

"See?" said Phil. "You stick with me, don't go marrying strangers."

"You're ridiculous, Phil. Darrell asked me to dinner, not to marry him."

Phil looked at Darrell. "Which was it? I don't seem to remember."

"I guess it was just dinner."

Phil nodded. "That was it. I remember now. I'm going to write a book: The Care and Feeding of T-Bone. The first chapter starts: 'To keep her pelt glossy and smooth, take a gallon of the finest cream'—"

"Phil! You clown!"

Phil looked across the room. "Brace yourselves."

Duff came into the bar, wearing flannel slacks, an old tweed hacking coat. His face was mottled, his eyes were round and hard and bright. He ignored Phil and Darrell. "Hello, T-Bone."

"Hello, Duff. I'm just going to bed."

"I thought you were going to bed hours ago."

"I was — but after I took the aspirin I felt better, so I went out."

"Oh? Where did you go?"

"Out to dinner. I was hungry. And now I'm going to bed."

"You could have called me. You had a date with me, remember?"

"But I had the headache! That's why I couldn't go!"

"So you had the headache. So you took the aspirin. So you went out. Why, then —"

"Duff, you get things so mixed up."

"Ha ha. We'll go tomorrow night instead. And —"

"I'm sorry, Duff. I can't. I'm going to dinner with Mr. Hutson."

"What? That be damned. I'm taking you to dinner."

"I've promised, Duff."

"You promised me last night for tonight."

"No, Duff." T-Bone was indignant. "I did no such thing! I said that —"

"Oh, never mind what you said. That's past and done. I'm talking about tomorrow night. Here's Hutson, you can break the date right now."

"Sh, Duff! Don't make a scene."

Phil said, "Duff, if you can't keep your voice down in here, you'd better leave."

"I'm not talking to you, Phil."

"I know you're not, but I hear you. These rows is getting to be an awful drag."

Duff lowered his voice. "All right. I'm talking quietly. But I mean what I say. You can break this engagement with Hutson. I'm sick of Hutson. Everywhere I look, there's Hutson."

"Duff, behave yourself."

"Will you do as I ask?"

"That's not a nice attitude to take," said T-Bone.

"Do you hear me, Hutson? You keep yourself clear. That means anything to do with this young lady."

Phil said, "Be sensible, Duff. Calm down."

"I will after I get this thing settled."

"It's something you can't settle. If T-Bone wants to go out with you, she'll go. If she doesn't want to, you can't bully her into it."

Duff stared at him cold-eyed. "I'll do without your advice. You can mind your own damned business if you please."

"I'm trying to."

Duff looked at Darrell. "Will you be good enough to tell T-Bone you're not taking her to dinner tomorrow night?"

Phil said, "Duff, I'd be careful if I were you. These quiet ones —"

Duff ignored him. "You heard what I said, Hutson. Tell her, if you will."

Darrell heaved a deep sigh. "Let's forget all this. It's like a bad dream. I'm in no mood to play."

Duff viciously sucked in his breath, edged forward. "That's of no matter to me."

"Outside!" cried Phil. "Outside!"

Duff started to the door, turned and waited. "Are you coming, Hutson?"

"Yes. Why not?"

They were followed by the usual crowd of sports-minded tipplers. Phil slipped out from under the bar. "I've got to watch this one myself."

T-Bone remained seated, her head drooping wistfully. Through the open door came sounds of conflict: hisses, grunts, the scuff of shoes on pavement. A muffled thud, louder than the others, then a drier more resonant sound. A brief period of silence. The thuds, bumps, hisses commenced again, somewhat slower in tempo. Then came a bass-drum thump, followed by a crisp wood-block effect. Again the silence. The noises recommenced, now rather deliberate. *Thump! Click! Bump!* Silence, quite profound.

Phil returned inside the bar. Shaking his head, he ducked under the counter. "I warned him. He sure got warned."

The tipplers returned to their stations; the Masquerade Bar sounded again: inconsequential chatter, the cheerful clink of bottle against glass. Darrell came unobtrusively back to his place. "I had a rather irritating day, I guess I took it out on Duff."

"Don't mention it. It's not your fault. Hell, it's not even Duff's fault. It's Miss Sizzlebritches here. She's been using Duff like a yo-yo, until the poor jerk is walking backwards."

"Phil, stop being so foolish. I'm going to bed. Really, this time." T-Bone gave her silky chestnut hair an indignant toss. She paused, turned rather hesitantly to Darrell. "Do you really want to take me to dinner?"

Behind the bar Phil croaked derisively. Darrell said, "Oh, yes. Certainly."

"About eight then?"

"Very well, eight o'clock."

T-Bone smiled briefly, departed into the lobby of the Balmoral. They heard her heels clicking up the marble steps.

"That's how it's done," said Phil. "That girl will never go hungry."

"Does she have any income at all?"

Phil wiped the bar industriously. "That's a matter of conjecture. I guess there's money seeping from somewhere: alimony, back taxes, blackmail. She makes a dollar here, a dollar there… She got one of her boy friends to buy a Jaguar; Mr. Burdette gave her a salesman's commission. Once in a while she sells a little dirt to her newspaper cronies. She models clothes once or twice a week. One way or another she makes out."

Darrell heaved a deep sigh. "Well, I'm off to bed too. Tomorrow…"

"Tomorrow what?"

"I don't know. I've come to a dead halt."

But as Darrell left the bar a familiar figure moved out of a shadowed doorway. "Mr. Hutson!"

"Well?"

"I saw you fight Mr. Mekkinesser. You pretty good fighter." Slip-Slip performed a series of rather inept feints and jabs. "Please don't never fight me."

Darrell turned to continue across the street but Slip-Slip protested. "Mr. Hutson, wait! Don't you want to know about Noel?"

"Have you found out anything?"

Slip-Slip nodded with solemn emphasis. "I talk to a man. Tomorrow morning he come to see you. Okay?"

"Okay," said Darrell. "Who is this man?"

"He's a good man. Maybe he knows something."

Darrell felt no large optimism. "Very well. I'll talk to him tomorrow."

"How much money you give?"

Darrell looked at him without friendliness. "How much money for what?"

"I work for you, I talk to this man."

"If I get any news of Noel you'll be paid. Well paid. You come see me later."

Slip-Slip smiled impishly. "Maybe better you give me money now."

"No. You see me tomorrow."

"You think I lie? You think the man don't come?"

"If I learn anything about Noel, you'll be paid."

Slip-Slip's grin faded slowly, like an afterglow.

Darrell asked, "What time does the man come?"

"In the morning. Early. Nine o'clock."

"Why haven't you told Mr. Upshaw about this man?"

"I don't understand, Mr. Hutson."

Darrell repeated the question.

Slip-Slip's face showed dubious comprehension. "They don't like me. They chase me off the boat. They think I'm bad guy. I'm not bad guy. I'm good guy. I work for you."

"That remains to be seen," said Darrell. "Well — at nine o'clock tomorrow."

"That's right. The man come to see you."

At nine the next morning the man came indeed: a thin Moroccan in a gray gabardine djellaba, a man with a shrewd tight face, a curious thin wedge of a nose. He looked into the lobby, saw Darrell, beckoned.

Darrell went out into the street. It was a beautiful morning, clear and cool, with sunlight pouring through the acacia trees. Darrell went to where the man stood beside the sun-burnt stucco wall of the hotel, watching with hard clever brown eyes. "Your name is Darrell Hutson?" He spoke English with the hard quick local accent.

"Yes."

"You looking for Noel Hutson?"

"Yes."

"You come with me." The Moroccan made a quick motion, started to walk away.

"Just a minute. Come back here."

The Moroccan stopped, motioned; then returned.

"We can talk here," said Darrell.

"No." The Moroccan shook his head decisively. "We go to Fez."

"To Fez! What for?"

"To see Jilali."

"Who is Jilali?"

"He is very important man. I take you to see him."

"Does Jilali know what's happened to Noel?"

"I take you, you ask him."

Darrell thought of Mohammed Ali Aktouf and his unpleasant death. Still, why should this happen to him? He had no irons in the fire; he knew nothing of guns or narcotics; he had no enemies among the Moroccans. On the other hand, what could Jilali tell him in Fez that could not be told here? Also, if someone had knowledge of Noel, why had they not taken it to Arthur Upshaw, who would pay at least as handsomely as Darrell?

There might be sensible answers to the questions, but Darrell could think of none. Which, of course, did not mean that answers did not exist. The essence of the matter was, that if he accompanied this hard-faced Moroccan to Fez, he was submitting himself to circumstances beyond his control, a process at which his instincts rebelled. Still, there it was; the only remaining possibility of learning something about Noel's disappearance. Take it or leave it.

He could take it — but also take precautions. He approached the Moroccan. "Let me see your identity card."

The man stared at him in silence, then brought out his card. The photograph was correct, the name read: Abd Allah el Kazim.

Darrell copied the name and the number of the card on the back of an envelope. "How are we going?"

Abd Allah el Kazim beckoned him to a small dusty Citroën. He entered, motioned Darrell toward the opposite side. "Just a minute," said Darrell. He made a note of the license number, returned to the hotel.

He went to the desk clerk, displayed the envelope. "See this number? It's the license of a car, a Citroën. I'm going to Fez with this man, Abd Allah el Kazim. This is the number of his identity card. If I'm not back here tomorrow take this to the police. Do you understand?"

The clerk dubiously accepted the envelope. Darrell made sure that his instructions were understood, and returned outside, half-expecting the Citroën to be gone.

But it had not moved. Darrell climbed in; el Kazim wordlessly started the motor. They rolled down Calle Miranda, turned up the hill, joined the coast highway, and presently left Tangier behind.

CHAPTER VIII

ABD ALLAH EL KAZIM drove hunched forward, chin almost resting on the wheel. Hostility was implicit in his silence. Evidence of baneful intent? Or the opposite? If he and Jilali meant harm, would they not take greater pains to hide their animosity? So Darrell reasoned, without conviction. Now that he was underway, he thought of a dozen precautions he should have taken: a visit to the police station, the company of a third party, insistence on learning more details before leaving Tangier. Well, the die was cast. Confound that cursed Noel.

Between Tangier and Fez lay three hundred kilometers, one hundred and ninety miles. El Kazim drove with the speedometer needle wavering between 80 and 90 kilometers per hour. They should arrive in Fez during the early afternoon.

They passed across a landscape of rolling hills, green with spring grass, patched with flowers. Here and there Moroccans cultivated fields using camels teamed with donkeys: a strange sight. Occasionally they passed a dingy village consisting of a gas pump, a fruit stand, a French-owned café, a huddle of mud huts.

El Kazim finally broke the silence. "You have never been to Fez?"

"No. This is my first visit to Morocco."

"Fez is a very old city, a holy city. Very interesting."

"So I should imagine."

They passed through another squalid village; el Kazim gestured toward the mud hovels. "You think the people are poor?"

"They seem to be."

"That is the fault of the French. They own everything in Morocco. They are everywhere, like ants, and carry everything away."

Darrell made no comment.

"There is much wealth in Morocco," said el Kazim, "but the people are poor. I tell you something very few Americans know; some day North Africa is rich!"

"I hope so," said Darrell. "I dislike poverty."

"But you do nothing to help us! You give the French money to buy guns; you help them kill the Moslems."

"That's not the intention," said Darrell. "We've also sent aid to Morocco."

"Do you know what the Russians will do for us? They are planning to help us, like brothers. They will make good water from the sea and build a great pipeline to take it into the middle of the Sahara. There will be a great lake, everything will be changed!"

Darrell laughed. "You don't believe that, do you? The project isn't possible."

El Kazim smiled thinly. "You would naturally say that."

"Yes. Because I'm a civil engineer. The plan is not practical. There's no basin for a Sahara lake in the first place. In the second no one knows how to remove salt from sea-water in the quantity necessary for such a lake."

El Kazim sniffed. Presently he asked, "What do Americans think of the Pan-Arab Union?"

"I suppose we feel it's the business of the countries involved," said Darrell.

"Then why do you help the French?"

Darrell laughed. "The French ask, 'Why do you help the Arabs?' It's like most human problems, rights and wrongs on both sides. I don't know the solution."

"When the French are pushed into the sea: that is the solution," said el Kazim grimly.

"If you can make it stick."

"The French can't resist the Moslem people. All North Africa will be Pan-Arab soon. Much sooner than you think. Nasser will do this. He is a great man! He is our George Washington!"

From the Moslem point of view, the analogy was by no means absurd, thought Darrell.

"What do you think?" challenged el Kazim. "Do you believe the French should own Algeria, that they should be rich while we are poor?"

Darrell hesitated. "Eventually I suppose all the states of the world will be organized into great territorial federations; I suppose in principle I'm in favor of the Pan-Arab Union. Although I can't say I care much for Nasser."

"Because he is a Moslem who spits in the Westerner's face."

"It's an unpleasant habit," Darrell remarked.

El Kazim made no reply; the conversation languished. The countryside became dry and harsh, the hills bleak. Eucalyptus occasionally lined the road; spiky white asphodel grew thick on the rocky slopes. They came to a junction: Rabat and Casablanca to the right, Meknes and Fez to the left. Without hesitation el Kazim swung left. The kilometer markers fell behind, the road looped up and over the low hills. Shortly after noon they reached Meknes, but passed through seeing no more than the main street of the French town. Leaving Meknes the road turned sharply northeast, and seemed to rise on a long slow slant. Far ahead a gray mass loomed along the horizon, the Atlas. They passed a kilometer marker, FEZ 60. Darrell calculated. Sixty kilometers, thirty-seven miles. An hour's drive.

The landscape was dull and ugly, the engine buzzed hypnotically, the hour passed swiftly. They entered the outskirts of Fez — small wind-softened houses of mud, commercial buildings of brick and corrugated metal. The road branched; el Kazim bore to the left, and the road became an alley, winding and bumping around the hillside, which appeared to be a great disheveled cemetery. To his right Darrell glimpsed the city, dust-colored, intricate as the cross section of a beehive, then a mud wall cut off his view. The road widened into a square, thronging with men, women, children, in djellabas rich and ragged, of white, off-white, drab, brown and gray; donkeys staggering under cruel loads; gaunt dogs. The square ended at a forty-foot wall pierced by an arched portal; here sat a row of beggars. El Kazim parked the car, jumped nimbly out. Darrell followed more slowly. "Where do we go now?"

"This is Bab Boujeloud. Bab means gate. It is the entrance to the medina. You come with me."

They passed through Bab Boujeloud into a narrow street. The crowd paid them no attention. The passage was paved with cobblestones, slippery where water trickled across, constricted by tall mud-brick walls. It wound, forked, joined, jerked aside in erratic doglegs, widened, narrowed, ducked under beamed archways. El Kazim turned right, left, right, left, left, left, right, apparently at random. They passed heavy doors of carved wood, blue-tiled fountains, small dark workshops. An irregular bar of blue sky followed overhead, and sometimes there was a glimpse of the sun. Occasionally the passage became a dark tunnel, thirty, forty or fifty feet long. Darrell became lost at once; the city was without pattern or form. Then, after twisting along a runway hardly wide enough for two persons to pass abreast, they emerged into a broad avenue. El Kazim turned through a gate; they stood in a large public garden planted with cypress, orange and lemon trees, rose bushes in full flower, privet hedges, banks of heliotrope and verbena, violets and pansies. A large colonnaded building of buff sandstone surrounded the garden on three sides. Moslems, as well as men and women in European clothes, strolled through the garden, passing into the rooms behind the colonnade.

Darrell looked about in puzzlement. "What are we doing here?"

"This is the Dar Batha. It is an old palace, now it is a museum. Come. I show you some interesting things."

Darrell asked, "Is this where we meet your friend?"

"He is not here. It is not time to see him. We go to the museum."

Darrell turned away, looked across the garden. Nothing, he thought, makes a person appear more foolish than helpless anger; to express his exasperation would only prompt el Kazim to amusement. "Very well," said Darrell with formal politeness. "If you wish to look at the museum, we shall do so."

"It is not for me," said el Kazim sharply. "It is for you!"

Darrell made a courteous gesture, implying that el Kazim should feel free to enjoy himself at his leisure. El Kazim's mouth compressed, his eyes shone. "Come," he said. "I show you some things."

In one of the halls hung an exhibition of contemporary Moroccan oil painting. Darrell, who had no particular interest in such matters, glanced around with perfunctory attention. So far as he could judge, the paintings seemed competently executed, after one or another of the conventional modern fashions.

El Kazim, however, was more enthusiastic. He walked here and there, looking from the paintings to Darrell, with eyes shining. "What do you think?" he demanded. "Are these not good?"

"They certainly seem to be," said Darrell.

"You see, we know these things as well as you," said el Kazim. "We are not ignorant natives!"

"I never imagined that you were," said Darrell.

"We look at other things," said el Kazim. He led the way through an armory displaying hundreds of Berber muskets, with short curved stocks and freakish long barrels. Another rack held daggers, stilettos, poniards, cutlasses — rows of shining steel blades, murderous points, symbols of hate and death.

El Kazim led Darrell into another chamber, this hung with ancient rugs and the brocaded robes of long-dead grandees. The center of the room was occupied by a cage, about three feet on a side, framed with heavy timbers, grilled with iron bars three-quarters of an inch in diameter. El Kazim seemed to find the cage interesting. He walked around it, peering into the cramped interior. "Look!" He pointed to a card. "Read!"

Darrell confessed his inability. "It's in French."

"It says that the cage was used in 1909 by the Sultan. He put a rebel inside until he died. Not nice, yes?"

"No. Not at all nice."

El Kazim laughed shortly, nodded in profound thought. He led Darrell into a room housing a collection of nondescript pottery. Darrell made not even the pretense of inspecting it.

El Kazim turned him a series of quick sardonic glances, then said, "Let's go see Jilali."

Once again they plunged into the fantastic complexity of the medina. They walked for twenty minutes, el Kazim never faltering, never pausing at a turning. It seemed impossible that he could know where he was going. Each corner was like every other; every passage and alley seemed identical to the one they had left. They passed through the spice market: a row of shops displaying in shallow bins heaps of paprika, nutmeg, saffron, cumin, pepper, turmeric. The colors burnt rich as paint pigments: ocher, vermilion, raw sienna, umber, cadmium orange, chrome yellow.

El Kazim struck off into a warren of dark winding passages smelling of carrion and ammonia, unpopulated except for anonymous huddles of rags, bone and gristle. He stopped beside a particularly scabrous wall, pounded on a heavy timber door.

The door was opened; an old woman peered out. El Kazim motioned, Darrell stepped into a small garden. Lemon trees clipped into perfect globes circled a fountain which sent up a dozen thin jets of water. Four identical cypresses marked the corners of a square, each cypress surrounded by a bed of violets. Pomegranates grew against the wall, roses climbed the columns of an arcade at the back of the garden.

The old woman retreated to the arcade, backed through a door. El Kazim motioned Darrell to follow. They entered a hall paved with elaborately patterned tiles. A door opened; a pale handsome man with striking black eyebrows, wearing a neat dark blue suit, bowed, moved politely back.

Darrell obeyed the implicit invitation, entered the room. El Kazim came behind him.

"This is Moulay Aziz ben Jilali," said el Kazim. "This is Mr. Hutson. Be seated, please."

Darrell looked from one man to the other. In Jilali's house, did el Kazim issue the orders? He settled himself gingerly on a low divan. A handsome red rug covered the floor; on the wall opposite hung a portrait of Gamal Abdel Nasser.

Jilali and el Kazim established themselves on a divan across the room. No one spoke. There was a long moment of silence.

Darrell stirred impatiently. "Mr. Jilali, I understand that you can give me news of my brother Noel."

Jilali made an uninterested gesture. "We will talk business soon. There is time. Did you enjoy your ride?"

"Very much. Morocco is an interesting country."

"Morocco is a great country," said Jilali.

The old woman hobbled in with a teapot, a bowl of sugar and three cups on a brass tray. There was further delay while the tea was poured.

Through a window Darrell could look out over the garden. There was no sound but the splash of the fountain.

Jilali spoke in a mild almost apologetic voice. "There are many such gardens in Fez. A man walking through the streets never knows what is behind the walls. Here in his house a man is truly a king."

Darrell drank his tea thoughtfully. An ominous hint? He had committed no offense against these people; they had no reason to wish him harm. And was not the Moslem code of hospitality extremely rigid, especially if the guest had broken bread? Still — they had served no bread.

"Fez is the oldest of the imperial cities," said Jilali. "It is one of the holy cities of Islam; students from everywhere come to study the Koran. Did el Kazim show you a *medersa*? A *medersa* is a college."

"No. We looked at other things."

Jilali nodded languidly. "Perhaps you will have another chance." He put down his cup. "It is good of you to come here."

"I am anxious to find my brother."

El Kazim spoke in Arabic; Jilali lazily put his hands behind his head, leaned back on the divan. "Good, we will talk."

"This is what we can tell you," said el Kazim rapidly. "Noel Hutson drove a truck with guns to a supply center for the Algerian National Army. It was the first of fourteen deliveries. By mistake he was given payment for the entire shipment, over forty tons of weapons. Returning to Tangier he met a group of French soldiers. Noel drove away from them. He feared capture, and hid the payment for the guns. But he was captured soon after. The French are cruel when they suspect that someone works to help make Algeria free. They beat Noel. He told them nothing. They put him in a cage — like the one you saw at the Dar Batha."

Darrell raised his eyebrows. "Strange that I should see just such a cage today."

El Kazim continued in a flat voice. "There is a man among the French who we pay. He told us they have Noel. We said, make him loose! No, he can not do that; it is a great risk. Not unless we pay much money. Too bad! We do not have the money. All our money is gone. If we find where Noel hid the payment, then we have much money, and Noel would go free."

Darrell leaned back, smiling bitterly. "You don't credit me with much intelligence."

El Kazim looked a trifle puzzled.

Jilali made a lazy remark in Arabic, and el Kazim turned back to Darrell. "You understand?" he asked sharply. "First we find the payment, then Noel is free from the French."

Either they take me for a fool, thought Darrell, or they think they're showing me the escape hatch, a way to save face. "I find it hard to believe that the French put Noel in a cage."

"No, no," said el Kazim vehemently. "They are cruel! It is never said in the newspapers what the French do."

Jilali sat up. He reached in his pocket, brought forth a photograph which he thrust at Darrell.

"This is the picture our friend made," said el Kazim in a formal voice. "It shows Noel in the cage."

Darrell studied the photograph. It undoubtedly depicted a man crouched within a cage, and the man's head was certainly that of Noel. Darrell examined the picture so carefully that Jilali became impatient and held out his hand. Darrell returned the picture. "I'm afraid your friend is deceiving you."

"What do you say?" asked el Kazim in a sharp voice.

"The picture is a fake."

Jilali and el Kazim stared at him: Jilali in reproach, el Kazim in waspish irritation.

"It is a photograph," said Jilali. "Is it not Noel?"

"Oh, it's Noel all right. And that's certainly a cage. But notice the shadows on the left side of Noel's face. The cage was photographed by flash from the front. Noel's face shows through the bars. Are they made of glass? Why is Noel smiling so happily? Because he feels secure?"

Jilali frowned down at the picture. El Kazim looked at Darrell with a hard smile. "Sometimes it is wrong to be too clever. The picture is not important. What you must do is tell us how to find the narcotic. Where is it?"

"I have no idea."

"You had a letter from your brother. This is our information. He must have told you."

"He told me nothing of the sort."

"It is very serious, Mr. Hutson. You realize?"

"Gentlemen, let's be reasonable." Darrell hitched himself forward on the divan. "I know you want to see the letter that Noel wrote home. I'm willing to show it to you in exchange for some information; in fact, that's the only reason I came to Fez, to make this exchange with you."

Jilali nodded thoughtfully and started to speak, but el Kazim thrust his arm out sharply. "So that you can help Noel escape with the narcotic!"

"No," said Darrell patiently. "Definitely not. I want nothing to do with it." He looked from el Kazim to Jilali. "Now — all this talk about cages aside — can you tell me anything about Noel? Is he alive or is he dead?"

El Kazim waited until Darrell had finished, the hostility now shining frankly and unpleasantly from his face. "We must ask about this letter. You have it with you?"

"No. It doesn't mention your heroin. If it did, I'd have turned it over to the police."

"Ah! Ah! Ah!" El Kazim leaned forward triumphantly. "Then you are against us!"

"I'm neither against you nor for you. I'm against traffic in narcotics."

"Then why have you and Noel made arrangement to sell the heroin?"

Darrell sighed, barely able to restrain his disgust. "You make everything so complicated. Believe me, I know nothing, care nothing for your business. If you can give me news of my brother, please do so; otherwise, I'd like to go back to Tangier."

Jilali spoke in Arabic, el Kazim nodded. He turned back to Darrell. "You are right, there is no need to be angry. Show us this letter, and we will take you to Tangier."

"If you'll tell me what you know of Noel."

"He has disappeared with our property; that is all we know. We wish to find him."

"But where did he disappear from? Who saw him last? Did he leave any message?"

El Kazim shook his head. "We can not tell these things. Perhaps you will tell the French…"

"No. I only want to find Noel and return to the States."

"Impossible. And now —"

Darrell struggled to keep his voice even. "You've brought me down here for nothing!"

"And now — the letter, please."

"I don't have it here. In any event it's a personal letter; it contains nothing to help you."

"I'm sorry, Mr. Hutson, we can not take your word for this. Will you stand up? I will search your pockets."

Darrell felt his muscles turn to stone.

El Kazim's voice came smoothly. "Please do not make trouble, Mr. Hutson. Please stand up. I do not want to call the servants. It is much easier if you help."

Darrell looked from one to the other. Jilali raised his fine black eyebrows in deprecation; el Kazim, grinning like a fox, stepped forward.

Burning with humiliation, furious with himself, but unwilling to make an issue of an inconsequentiality, Darrell rose to his feet. El Kazim patted his pockets, extracted his wallet, his passport, a few miscellaneous odds and ends. Jilali watched, mouth drooping in annoyance.

"Where is the letter?" asked el Kazim. "In your hotel?"

"No."

Jilali uttered a terse sentence in Arabic; el Kazim sat back. "I must explain this carefully, so you will see exactly how important is this letter. Please sit down."

Darrell resumed his seat on the divan.

"There is a large shipment of weapons at Tangier. It is ours. We sent the heroin to pay for it. No, do not look in disgust. The heroin will be sold in Paris. Is that not justice? That the French who try to make slaves of us should pay for our guns? No matter. We do not care for right or wrong. We have one truckload of the weapons. We cannot have the others until we pay for them. But this is now impossible. The heroin comes across the desert from Egypt, a long way, very dangerous, very expensive. A million dollars, it is worth so much. I am what you call the purchase agent; the heroin is in my charge, and they say it is my blame. I do not want the blame. So you help us, and there is no blame. Even if

THE MAN IN THE CAGE

you do not want to help us, you must. I have explained that this is very serious. Do you understand?"

"Yes. I understand."

"Where is the letter?"

"It is in the mail."

"The post office? You put it in the post?"

"Yes."

Jilali spoke in Arabic; el Kazim responded, then turned back to Darrell. "Where did you send this letter?"

Darrell weighed his answer. It would be simple to tell them an untruth; they could not disprove it. He thought of Aktouf, the desk clerk. Let them have the letter, which after all could tell them nothing. It was folly to make himself trouble merely because he resented coercion.

El Kazim and Jilali watched him keenly.

"I mailed the letter to myself," said Darrell. "Care of American Express."

"In Tangier?"

"Yes, in Tangier."

"Good," said el Kazim. Jilali clapped his hands; a sour-faced Negro servant appeared. Jilali gave orders.

"You will write to American Express," said el Kazim. "You must tell them to give your letter to the man who brings your passport. Then you must wait here till I get the letter."

Darrell sat still. The request followed from what had gone before; but enough was enough. Too much. He rose to his feet, leaned forward, took the passport. "I'll show you the letter. But I'll keep my own passport."

Jilali's raven-wing eyebrows rose, his mouth drooped in distress. El Kazim, however, smiled. "Please, Mr. Hutson, do not make trouble. This will be done as we think best."

"You take me back to Tangier; tomorrow I'll get you the letter. You have my word on that. I don't see any reason why I should stay here."

Jilali spoke in Arabic, apparently a counsel of moderation; el Kazim remonstrated, gesticulating with his fingers. Jilali shrugged.

"I am sorry," said el Kazim. "Perhaps you will change your mind. It is better that you write the letter."

Darrell turned, walked from the room, started down the hall. Behind him came el Kazim's voice, "If you go into the garden I will shoot you."

Darrell stopped short, looked back. El Kazim held an automatic pistol aimed at his middle. He spoke through a tight smile. "Come back, please."

Darrell slowly returned, feeling rather more comfortable. The situation was less damaging to his self-respect; he was submitting not to browbeating, but to the universal language of the bullet. El Kazim, by the same token, had become angry; he had enjoyed humiliating the American; he had relished the understated menaces and silken hints. Now he had become secondary to the gun.

He motioned Darrell back toward the divan. Jilali had not moved, and watched with resignation as el Kazim prodded Darrell with the gun. "Please sit." He thrust forward paper and a ball-point pen. "Write: 'Please give all my letters to the man who shows you my passport.' Sign it."

Darrell wrote. El Kazim took the letter, scrutinized it carefully. "Your passport."

Darrell wordlessly handed it over.

"Thank you. Now, please stand up."

Jilali spoke in Arabic; el Kazim responded emphatically. Darrell looked from one to the other. Jilali seemed to have nominal authority, but el Kazim, exerting greater energy, set the mood of the situation. El Kazim had the last word; Jilali gave a sour-faced shrug. El Kazim waved the gun. "Go to the door, turn to the right, walk to the far end of the hall."

Darrell did as instructed, walking until a door of heavy planks barred the way.

"Open the door."

Darrell pushed the door open.

"Go in."

Darrell entered a large dim room smelling of straw and damp wood, evidently at one time a stable. Massive plank doors on iron hinges hung on the wall opposite; a pair of high windows admitted late-afternoon light through panes clouded with dust and spider webs.

The room now served other purposes than the shelter of donkeys. In the center of the straw-littered floor was a cage, almost identical to the one Darrell had seen in the museum.

He stared at it. At his back el Kazim said in a voice which had regained its fluency, "We have no nice way to keep you safe. So we will put you in the cage for tonight. Tomorrow, if all goes well, you will be allowed to go free."

Darrell slowly turned, stared into el Kazim's hard brown eyes. In the gloating, the triumph, the unreasoning malice, he saw the new face of the East; he knew that he was making atonement for centuries of enforced obsequiousness. "You force me to take sides," said Darrell. "I'm sure now that I don't care for the Pan-Arab Union."

"What you care makes no difference. We will cleanse Africa; we will drive you into the sea. You think you are better than we are, with your pink bellies and painted women. You are rich and fat and weak; we are poor and strong. We shall see who wins. Into the cage."

Darrell looked at the cage. It was no larger than a dog kennel. The top was hinged back; el Kazim evidently intended that he should step inside and crouch. El Kazim then would slam down the lid.

El Kazim said, "If you don't enter the cage —" he reached to the floor, picked up a loose coil of rope "— I will call the servant and he will tie you. Hurry!"

"This is simply fantastic," muttered Darrell. "Do you think you can —"

"Into the cage! Or do you prefer the rope!"

Darrell stifled the useless words which rose to his tongue, along with his pride. He went sideways to the cage, hoping that el Kazim would offer him a chance to seize the gun. But el Kazim stood well away.

He raised a leg, straddled the side of the cage. El Kazim came a step closer. Darrell slowly drew his other leg over.

"Down," rasped el Kazim throatily.

Darrell slowly lowered himself. El Kazim's expression sickened him. It would mean real danger to thwart him in his present excitement. He squatted on his haunches. El Kazim approached with long elastic strides, slammed down the lid to the cage. Darrell ducked. The impact vibrated the bars, rang through his head. The padlock clicked. El Kazim backed away, tucking the gun into his pocket.

"You thought the picture of your brother in the cage was false? So it was. If he were in the cage he would not be smiling."

"Where is Noel?" asked Darrell, as if the question had only just occurred to him.

El Kazim grinned. "I do not know. But we will find him. Do you know something? He killed my brother; it is right that you should suffer something. Be thankful that I do not shoot you. Be thankful that the cage is all you suffer!"

Darrell said nothing. El Kazim watched him another ten seconds, then went to the door. He turned for one last look, then departed. The door slammed shut; Darrell was alone, hunched in the cage, arms across his knees. He blew out his breath in enormous annoyance. "This is incredible…Noel, wherever you are, I'd be very happy if you were here instead of me."

He changed his position, leaned back against the bars, knees spraddled to the side. He looked at his watch. Six o'clock. When Noel learned of this, he would laugh with vast merriment. Everyone else would laugh too. Noel calls for succor, Darrell comes gallantly to the rescue, and is clapped into a cage…Where the devil was Noel? Paris? The Riviera? Capri? Darrell's assurance wavered. Everyone else might be right and he wrong. Perhaps Noel indeed had fled with the loot. And meanwhile Darrell crouched in a cage…He looked at his watch again. One minute after six. It would be a long night.

CHAPTER IX

DARRELL SHIFTED HIS POSITION several times. For the twentieth time he looked at his watch. Seventeen minutes had passed. Fury rose up in him, choking in his throat, like vomit. He gave a faint hoarse cry of passion, then, instantly ashamed, crouched back against the bars. Was there no way he could free himself from this damnable cage?

He pulled at one of the bars. It was soft wrought iron, about three-quarters of an inch in diameter, and gave a fraction of an inch under the strain. He pulled with every ounce he could muster, but the bar, fixed at top and bottom in the timber frame, only quivered. Darrell relaxed. Nineteen minutes had passed.

Perhaps el Kazim would sleep in Fez tonight, and not make the journey to Tangier until tomorrow, which meant an additional twelve hours in the cage. Darrell's detestation for Abd Allah el Kazim surpassed any emotion he had previously felt. He took hold of a bar once more, tugged till his throat corded. He doubled himself up, pushed with his feet. The bar gave slightly, until its tensile strength resisted further bending.

He examined the timber above and below. It was weathered and old and possibly a little rotten, but proof against any exertion of his muscles. He thought of the tools accessible at home: hydraulic jacks, air chisels, bolt cutters, oxyacetylene torches. Even with a hacksaw, a keyhole saw, any variety of saw, he could work himself free. In the dusty light seeping through the windows he searched the room. Since el Kazim and Jilali were not fools, they would leave no useful implement within his reach. As he expected, the stable offered him no assistance. A heap of firewood occupied one corner; rotting straps, blankets and donkey harness hung from pegs. A few odds and ends were visible — bottles, boxes, a threadbare automobile tire, the coil of rope with which el Kazim had offered to tie him, a stack of cracked dishes. Darrell's eyes fixed on the rope. A resourceful man could accomplish marvels with a length of rope. But he could not reach across the twenty feet intervening.

Darrell considered. He could tear his shirt into strips, knot the strips together, tie his shoe to the end, cast and drag the rope to him. Feasible, but perhaps there was another method which would spare him his shirt. He tried to rock the cage. It was very heavy; with his utmost exertion he could do little more than jar it. He rearranged himself within the cage, worked his foot through the hole in the floor. He put his back under the top of the cage. Heave, thrust. The cage raised, slid an inch; the edge of the hole banged against his ankle. Heave, thrust. Two inches…Ten minutes later Darrell obtained possession of the rope. The light was fading fast, and Darrell worked with all haste. He made a loop, cast it at the pile of firewood, and after several attempts managed to drag over a stout stick something over a foot long. "Now we shall see," thought Darrell. An engineering degree, plus six years of hard work and a certain amount of ordinary horse sense, should prove of some advantage.

But he hesitated, looking toward the door. Suppose el Kazim came to inspect him before leaving for Fez? Suppose the servant brought food? They would notice that the cage had been moved; they would investigate and take away the rope. Cursing and sweating, Darrell worked his foot through the hole, humped the cage inch by inch back across the floor to its original position.

He rested, easing the strain in his back, massaging his bruised ankle. He listened: no sound. He could wait until dark or try now… He lacked the patience to wait; it would have to be now.

He selected a bar on one side of the cage. He took the end of the rope around it, back through and across the cage, around three bars opposite, then back across, around the original bar, making a triangular circuit. He repeated the process four times, drew the rope tight, tied a knot. He inserted the stick into the triangle, between the two sets of strands, began to twist. Around and around. The ropes tightened; turning became hard. The bar bent, pulled inward. Darrell unwound the rope, took in the slack, and for greater margin of strength, added two more circuits. He started winding again. The bar bent, the timber creaked. The winding became difficult. Darrell loosened, took in the slack, began twisting again. The tension became very great; Darrell turned slowly, cautiously. There was a sharp snap of splitting wood, the twisting came suddenly easy; he had pulled the top end of the bar through the timber.

"One down," said Darrell. "Two, or possibly three to go."

Hurriedly he untied his rope, repeated the process on the next bar; this came more easily, for the timber had been split. A third bar and a fourth; and now by dint of twisting, bending, pulling, he made a gap large enough to crawl through.

He rose to his feet, stretched his cramped muscles. So much for the cage. Now to leave the house. He went to the doors which communicated with the street; they were barred, solid as the walls. In the gray dusk he could see a pair of enormous iron locks. He went to the door through which he had entered. This was also locked, but seemed less substantial than the outer doors.

He put his ear to the keyhole and seemed to hear a faint murmur of voices. He could not force the door without attracting attention.

He looked up at the windows. No great problem here. He dragged the cage under the window. It made a soft scraping sound which Darrell hoped could not be heard outside the room. Then boxes: two small ones side by side, a larger one on top. Darrell gingerly climbed on top, explored for the window hardware. It was nonexistent; the windows were set solidly into the wall.

He jumped down, folded an old blanket, tossed it to the top of his makeshift ladder. He tied one end of the rope to the cage, clambered back up, carried the coil to the wide mud windowsill.

Now he was ready. He peered through the window, unsuccessfully trying to look down into the street. There was no reason to hesitate. He raised the folded blanket, held it against the pane, struck it with his fist. Glass tinkled, clattered below.

Darrell removed the blanket, put his head out. He looked into a passage only fifty feet long, quite deserted. He pushed the rest of the glass into the street, laid the blanket over the sash, threw out the rope. Then, crawling after the rope, he lowered himself to the street.

He stretched his arms, laughing in exultation. His ankle throbbed, his back ached, but these were minor considerations. He was free. Now, to find his way out of the maze. He had not the remotest notion of his location, or the distance to the nearest gate. On his way in he had seen nothing like a main street or thoroughfare, nothing but the incredible capillary system of passages and alleys.

He felt in his pockets and found about a thousand francs in loose change. Enough to hire a guide. El Kazim had mentioned the name of the gate by which they had entered: Bab Bou — something. Bab meant gate, which might be enough.

He set forth along passages now dimly illuminated with bare bulbs. Few people were abroad, and these looked at him suspiciously. Somewhere he had read that Christians were unwelcome in Moslem cities after sunset. If this were true, it could not be helped, and he was quite willing to leave. He passed a thin-faced boy of sixteen, stopped him, pointed to himself, then away. "Bab? You take me to bab?" He reached in his pocket, brought out two hundred francs. "I want to go to the bab."

The boy backed away, rubbing his nose in puzzlement.

"Bab." Darrell pointed in various directions. "Bab?"

The boy smiled with the easy superiority of the metropolitan for the rustic. He pointed. "Bab Ftouh." He pointed in another direction. "Bab Boujeloud."

Darrell nodded. "Bab Boujeloud." He took the boy's arm. "Come. Bab Boujeloud. You show me. Two hundred francs."

The boy at last comprehended the nature of Darrell's requirements, and became full of an excited officiousness, running ahead, gesturing. Darrell saw that he had selected a half-wit for his guide. "The blind leading the blind," he told himself. "Lead on, I'm not proud, so long as we arrive."

With the boy prancing and skipping ahead, Darrell plodded back through the warren of the Fez medina. The boy was not content merely to lead; he felt it necessary to assure Darrell that they were approaching their destination, beckoning, pointing, hopping backwards. When they came to the more populous streets Darrell began to feel conspicuous. The boy felt only pride in his occupation. Darrell doggedly marched after him, and at last was rewarded by the sight of the massive wall, the tall pointed-arch gate.

The boy led him to the opening, took the two hundred francs and departed. Darrell walked out into the open area, past the spot where el Kazim had parked the Citroën. The place was now vacant. Evidently el Kazim was on his way to Tangier.

Fifty yards beyond he found a taxi stand. He went to the first in line. *"Taxi, monsieur?"* called the driver.

"Yes," said Darrell. "I want to go to Tangier."

"Tangier?" the driver asked in mingled doubt and suspicion. *"Beaucoup d'argent, monsieur."*

"I expect so," said Darrell. He opened the door, flung himself wearily into the seat. "Nevertheless — Tangier."

The driver scrutinized him over the back of the seat. An American, hence a millionaire, either mad or drunk. "Tangier, *monsieur?*"

"Tangier."

The driver shrugged: a fare was a fare. He got out of the cab, spoke to one of his fellows, then returned. He started the motor, swung around and set forth.

Sometime after midnight the cab swung over the hill and down into the bright amphitheater of Tangier. Darrell roused himself, directed the driver to the Masquerade Bar.

Here the night was young. A babble of conversation and laughter issued through the door, the brass globes spattered color against the windows. Darrell motioned the driver to follow him inside. Booths and bar were crowded. Mr. Burdette occupied his favorite stool near the end of the bar, drinking with the chesty young matron, who called him "Dolling" in an abominable froglike croak. Behind the bar Phil Beresford worked, talked, laughed, drank, exchanged quips with old friends, welcomed newcomers, wished Godspeed to those departing, took orders, mixed drinks, collected funds, punched the cash register, opened bottles, cracked ice. Tonight he wore a mint-green sport coat, dark green gabardine slacks, a dark green silk tie. Darrell attracted his attention. "Good evening, kind sir," called Phil. "Where you been? T-Bone thought famine had struck when you failed to show up."

"T-Bone? I forgot all about her." He drew Phil to the side. "I lost my wallet. Will you pay the cab for me? A loan until tomorrow."

"Delighted. This the man? How much?"

"I don't know. I don't speak his language. All the way from Fez."

Phil's eyebrows rose. "From Fez by taxi? That's like coming down from London on the Royal Barge. Well, well, well." He settled with the driver, returned to Darrell. "Fifteen thousand francs. About thirty bucks. Not too bad."

"Give him an extra thousand and a drink if he wants one."

The driver declined the drink, took the money, departed.

Darrell found an empty stool, seated himself. "Is the kitchen still open? I'm starving."

"From two in the afternoon till two at night."

"I want a steak the size of a suitcase. I haven't eaten since breakfast."

"Sure thing. Here, come down to this end of the bar, next to Mr. Burdette, where it's a little handier. Something to drink?"

"I'll have a highball. One for you?"

"As usual."

Mrs. Phil presently sailed in from the kitchen with the steak, her face placid and remote. She strutted past Phil as if he were nonexistent, put down the plate, departed.

Mr. Burdette addressed Darrell in a voice loud enough for Phil to hear. "Notice Phil's new outfit? Pretty gay, what?"

Phil regarded Mr. Burdette in hurt amazement. "Sure it's gay. Why not?"

"Business must be picking up," Mr. Burdette told Darrell. "I saw Mrs. Phil pricing a mink coat today."

"Mink fertilizer for the African violets, more likely."

Mr. Burdette winked at Darrell. "African violets! What a lovely hobby!"

"After the first acre it gets old," grumbled Phil. "I'm willing to quit right now."

"Marriage is give and take, Phil."

"Don't get me wrong! I don't mind a plant here and there. But you can't let it get to be a mania. One day I had to pull apart the leaves at the window to see if the sun was shining. I told her, 'This is it! Get rid of this jungle or I'm gonna hack me a clearing with my machete!' So she crammed the whole works into her room. I don't know where she sleeps."

"I often wonder why and how you got married," mused Mr. Burdette.

"That's something I don't like to talk about," said Phil. "Still — since you're courtin' Mama — I guess you got a right to know. Just don't pass it on. We both come from the same town, Atlanta, Georgia. Mama got herself put on the draft board. One day she told me, 'You know something? Tomorrow we call in a new selection, all the single men whose initials is P.R.B.' My middle name being Roger, I took the hint. Sometimes I think I'd been better off in the paratroops."

Mr. Burdette loomed around the bar. "Speaking of Mama, where is lovely young T-Bone tonight?"

"Last I seen of her," said Phil, "she was out sitting on the curb, waiting for Darrell. How that girl loves to eat. I used to bait her once in awhile. But the last sandwich I ordered for her, Mama put in a long black hair."

"Aha! Jealousy!"

Phil shook his head. "Mama's not jealous. She's got her African violets. She just don't like T-Bone."

"Telephone," said Mrs. Phil, from a point two feet behind Phil. "For Mr. Burdette."

"Oh yes, of course." Mr. Burdette slid down from his stool, in the manner of a seal leaving an ice floe. "Excuse me." He trotted around behind the bar and into the kitchen.

Phil watched him with a knowing grin. "T-Bone, bah! Mr. Burdette's wooing Mama. He's the only man she allows in the kitchen, including me. And he always comes out chewing."

Mr. Burdette presently emerged, popping a last morsel into his mouth. The chesty young matron bellowed, "Dolling, dolling!" Mr. Burdette looked around. "Come along, dolling. We're all going. If you want to come, that is."

"Oh yes," called Mr. Burdette reedily. "Don't leave me here." He departed.

Phil came down the bar to Darrell. "See what I mean about the kitchen? He fascinates Mama with his African violet lore, and while she's daydreaming he fries himself a steak."

"What's he do for a living?"

"Automobile agency. He sold Ellen McKinstry that black engine of wrath. All he's got to do now is collect his money. How's the chow?"

"Only half enough. Otherwise fine."

"Want more? I hate to see a man go hungry. How about some pie?"

"I better settle for the pie."

Phil brought the pie himself. "You eat like you had an eventful day."

"I talked to some men in Fez."

"Learn anything?"

"Nothing much."

Darrell finished the pie, hoisted himself wearily to his feet. "I'm going to bed. I'll settle my bill tomorrow. Or as soon as I get a wire from home."

"Your credit's good."

Darrell went to the door. He looked up and down the street. The night was quiet. Wind rustled the acacia leaves; street lights blinked and flickered through the foliage. A few forlorn shop windows glowed on empty sidewalks; a dozen cars stood desolate along the curb.

Darrell crossed the street, entered the hotel. At the desk he left a call for eight o'clock, climbed the stairs to his room. He took a hot shower, went to bed.

For a long time he lay staring into the dark. If he had not been able to reach the rope! At this moment he would be sitting in the cage, hunched, cramped, aching…They must know by now that he got away; Jilali or a servant would have brought in food and drink. They might or might not have been able to inform el Kazim; el Kazim might or might not show himself in the morning.

The American Express office opened at nine. Darrell would be there. He hoped that el Kazim would be there too. He smiled in the dark, and presently fell asleep.

CHAPTER X

THE MORNING WAS FRESH and clear; Tangier sparkled like a bowl of crushed ice. The streets sounded to the squeal of tires, voices in a dozen languages. Tourists and Tangerines mingled along the Boulevard Pasteur, each marveling at the whimsies of the other.

At twenty minutes to nine Darrell posted himself in a doorway across the street from the American Express office. Not the optimum situation, but if el Kazim presented himself at the crack of nine, there would be no time for Darrell to enter, explain matters to the company officials. El Kazim might look in the doorway, see Darrell and depart, taking the passport with him.

Minutes passed; the hour of nine arrived. A man in a brown suit — clearly a company official — stopped by the door, put a key in the lock, entered. Darrell stood looking up and down the street, watching for the flash of gray gabardine.

At four minutes after nine Abd Allah el Kazim appeared, striding briskly from the direction of the Arab Quarter. Beside him, to Darrell's surprise, walked Jilali, dapper and handsome in his neat black suit.

They approached the door with assurance. Darrell, observing their calm faces, burned with fury. Sauntering at their ease, they believed him in Fez, crouched in the cage.

Jilali opened the door; el Kazim marched in looking neither right nor left, with Jilali at his heels.

Darrell crossed the street, went to the door, looked into the office. The man in the brown suit was coming forward from the rear. El Kazim tendered him the note Darrell had written.

Someone came up behind Darrell — a clerk arriving for work. He gave Darrell a curious glance, opened the door, entered. Jilali looked around at the clerk, turned back. Darrell stepped in before the door closed.

The man in the brown suit was reading the letter, scratching his cheek with a thoughtful finger. He spoke; el Kazim tossed the passport down on the counter.

Darrell stepped forward. El Kazim turned his head; the hard round brown eyes stared. He turned swiftly, reached for the passport. Darrell clutched his wrist, ground his fingers into the bones, took the passport.

The man in the brown suit stood back in alarm. "What is this, what is this?"

Darrell said, "I decided to come for my own mail. I am Darrell Hutson. This is my passport." He turned to el Kazim. "Give me my wallet."

El Kazim turned and started for the door; Darrell caught the hood of the gabardine djellaba, jerked him back. El Kazim wheeled, stood glaring like a hawk. "My wallet," said Darrell. "Or I'll call the police."

Jilali, without loss of dignity, reached into the breast pocket of his black coat, brought forth Darrell's wallet. "We do not rob you," he said in an injured voice.

Darrell looked inside the wallet; so far as he could judge his money was secure. The Moroccans started from the office. "Just a minute," said Darrell. "We've got a few things to talk about."

Jilali paused uncertainly by the door. El Kazim whirled himself furiously out into the street.

The official in the brown suit had been first leaning forward in agitation, then standing back in frozen-faced disapproval. "Is this a police matter? Do they rob you, sir? I will call the police!"

"No," said Darrell. "It is a mistake. Please see if I have any mail."

The man indecisively went to the mailbox, brought out a single letter. "Darrell Hutson."

"Yes, that's right. Thank you."

He went outside, followed by Jilali. El Kazim glowered from a hundred feet away.

Darrell spoke in a brittle voice. "Do you know why I haven't brought the police? There's only one reason. I want to find my brother. Do you understand?"

Jilali raised his handsome black eyebrows in reproach.

"I'll make a bargain with you. The same I went to Fez to make. You answer my questions and I'll show you this letter."

"What questions?" Jilali asked guardedly. "What do you want to know?"

"Only things that will help me find Noel."

El Kazim, fascinated against his will, returned step by reluctant step.

"Well, do you agree?" asked Darrell. "If not, I'll call the police."

Jilali looked toward el Kazim, jerked his head. The two spoke in Arabic. El Kazim looked sidewise at Darrell. "Come with us."

Darrell laughed in bitter amusement. "Not much chance of that."

Jilali said, "It is wrong to talk like this. We meant only to keep you safe. We want to win our great war. One man, two men — it is nothing."

"Will you answer my questions?"

"You must ask the questions. Perhaps I will answer."

"If you don't answer, I won't show you the letter, and I'll turn you over to the police. Come over here." Darrell led them a few yards up the side street.

El Kazim held out his hand. "You must show us the letter first."

"You talk like a fool," said Darrell contemptuously.

Jilali restrained el Kazim's retort with an impatient gesture. "Ask the questions."

"Noel left Tangier on the night of March ninth with a truckload of guns. Where did he go?"

El Kazim said harshly, "We cannot tell you these things."

"What is the difference?" asked Jilali. "The French know that guns come to somewhere near Taouz."

"Taouz? Where is Taouz?"

"It is a village in the Tafilelt near the Algerian border — a caravan station."

"Noel brought the truck to Taouz. Then what?"

"The arms were unloaded. Then there was a mistake. We had brought the payment across the desert from Egypt. But the sheikh at Taouz was afraid the French would come, and sent it with Noel and Habdid el Kazim to Tangier. On the road they fought. Noel killed Habdid el Kazim."

Abd Allah el Kazim thrust himself forward. "He threw him from the truck like a piece of refuse! Your brother did this to my brother!"

Darrell ignored him. "Go on," he said to Jilali.

"Noel drove to Erfoud. He went to the hotel there. The French call it the Gîte d'Etape. He stayed there over the night. He wrote a letter and he made two telephone calls to Tangier. The next morning a telephone call came to him. But already he had left the Gîte and no one knows where he went, or where is the payment for the guns."

"And that's all you know of Noel?"

"That is all we know."

"He made two telephone calls, you say?"

"That is our information."

"Who did he call?"

"We do not know. We have made questions at Erfoud. Noel asked for Arthur Upshaw, and spoke to someone who answered the call."

Darrell looked sidewise at el Kazim. "That man might have been Aktouf, the desk clerk at the Balmoral."

"We thought so," said Jilali in a neutral voice.

"You don't think so now."

"No."

"You tortured him to death to find out."

El Kazim could not restrain himself. "He was the most detestable of all swine. He was an Arab who hated his people, an Arab who loved the French. He was filth, he was unclean, with my two hands —" he showed Darrell a pair of quivering hands "— I would tear the throat of all these French-loving curs!"

"This matter does not concern you or your brother," said Jilali shortly.

"Did you send me a newspaper clipping describing Aktouf's death?"

Jilali and el Kazim both looked puzzled. "You were sent this clipping? By whom?"

"I don't know."

Jilali shrugged. "Do you have any more questions?"

"No." He handed Jilali the letter. El Kazim snatched it, ripped it open, held it to the light. They read laboriously, then reread, looked up with eyes that were puzzled and hurt, as if Darrell had deceived them. "But there is nothing here," said Jilali.

"I told you there was nothing."

"Then why did you conceal it? Why did you put it into the mail?"

"Because the people who wanted to read it would tell me nothing in return."

The two Moroccans read the letter once more. "What is 'copper my bets'?"

"I won't tell you. That's half an inch past the edge of the bargain. I wouldn't give you a quarter-inch. You put me in a cage, remember? For no reason whatever."

"Your brother killed a good Moslem! My brother!" grated el Kazim.

Jilali signaled him to quiet. "I wish to copy this."

"Go ahead."

Jilali made a careful copy on the back of an envelope, then returned the letter. The two Moroccans looked at each other, listless with disappointment.

"One more thing," said Darrell. "You took me on a wild goose chase to Fez."

"A — what you say?"

"You took me on a useless journey to Fez. You owe me fifteen thousand francs for my taxi fare back to Tangier."

El Kazim blew scornfully between his teeth. "That is your fault. Your letter told us nothing. It was not worth the trouble of speaking to you."

"You had no need to drive me to Fez. You could have spoken to me here. But you took me to Fez, and I had to spend fifteen thousand francs to get back. I want it returned."

"You will not get it from us." They turned and without further ceremony set off down the street.

Darrell looked at Noel's letter. "Copper my bets" — what the devil did he mean? The letter hinted much, told little… There was a tugging at his sleeve. Darrell swung around. Slip-Slip jerked back with great agility. He slowly approached, smiling archly.

"I'm glad to see you, Mr. Hutson. Maybe now you give me the money."

"Money? For what?"

"I say the man come at nine o'clock. You don't believe me. I work to bring the man."

"You brought him all right. He cost me fifteen thousand francs. Not to mention one or two other items. Get lost."

Slip-Slip shook his head dolefully. "I work for you. Now you don't pay!"

Darrell started back up the Boulevard Pasteur. Slip-Slip came after him. "What you want me to do, Mr. Hutson? I do what you want."

A sign attracted Darrell's attention: OFFICIAL MOROCCAN TOURIST BUREAU. He crossed the street, entered the building so designated, to emerge a few minutes later with a dozen maps and folders.

Slip-Slip was waiting for him. "You want to go for a ride? I know where is a good car. Cheap. Good car."

"No, thanks."

"I'm good guide."

"I don't need a guide." Darrell walked up the Boulevard Pasteur, leaving Slip-Slip staring disconsolately after him. In the Place de France he took a seat at a sidewalk café, ordered coffee. Shoe-shine boys converged like sharks on bloody meat. Darrell rebuffed them, waved away the nasturtium-colored silk scarfs, the rubber tarantulas, the jewelry, wrist watches and skull-caps, refused to inspect lewd photographs, and presently was allowed to sip his coffee in peace.

He unfolded a map, located Erfoud. It lay across the Middle Atlas, on the brink of the Sahara. The road led past Erfoud to a smaller village, Rissani. Another road, hardly more than a track, led to Taouz, almost against the Algerian border. The road by which Noel must have returned from Erfoud led to a town called Ksar-es-Souk. Here he could have turned either southwest toward Ouarzazate, and eventually Marrakech and Casablanca, or north toward Meknes and Tangier. Somewhere he must have halted for fuel. By now the trail would be cold, but there was a bare chance that someone would remember Noel. Or even the truck, especially if it had some distinguishing feature.

Darrell tried to deduce Noel's probable halting-places. The truck undoubtedly had left Tangier with a full tank of gas, and more than likely Noel had filled up again at Meknes. Returning from Erfoud he would refuel at Ksar-es-Souk, if facilities were available. Much depended on the fuel capacity of the truck. Arthur Upshaw could furnish this information, should he choose to do so. Darrell thought this highly unlikely. It would be equally futile to expect cooperation from Duff. Ellen could hardly be expected to know the cruising range of the truck, but she possibly could tell him its make and where it had been bought, what it looked like.

Darrell considered. To telephone Ellen carried the risk of an embarrassing rebuff. Nevertheless…Why not? He telephoned from a nearby drug store.

Ellen showed the least possible cordiality when he identified himself. "Are you very busy?" he asked.

"Why?"

"I want to talk to you."

"About Noel, I suppose."

"Yes, I'm afraid so."

"I'm not interested. I'm busy packing, as well."

"Packing? Why?"

"The house is no longer ours."

"Oh. I should think then you'd want to help me find Noel." Darrell felt an immediate pang of guilt, for he seemed to imply that she, Duff and Arthur Upshaw were entitled to a million dollars' worth of heroin. Through familiarity, the shipment was losing its flavor of evil.

"I'm sick of the name Noel," said Ellen. "I'm sick of the name Hutson."

"Well, answer a question or two for me. I've learned that Noel left Tangier in a truck."

"A lorry."

"A lorry, then. What make of lorry? What color?"

"I don't know what make. Why do you want to know?"

"I'm going to Erfoud to make inquiries. I want to know what to inquire for."

"So you found out about Erfoud." Ellen's voice became thoughtful. "How?"

"That's a long story."

There was a pause. Then she asked, "Where are you now?"

"The Place de France."

"I'll be down in five minutes."

"Make it ten. I'd rather you didn't kill yourself."

"Oh you would, would you?" Ellen's voice was neutral. "I won't be long, in any case."

Darrell hung up the telephone, went out to stand on the sidewalk.

Eight minutes passed, then up the street prowled the drooping snout of the Mercedes-Benz, with Ellen's tawny head behind the windscreen. She stopped, Darrell jumped in beside her. The motor throbbed and they were away.

"Where are we going?" he asked.

"Nowhere particular." On this warm sunny day Ellen wore a pair of white tennis shorts, a white blouse, old white sneakers. Darrell averted his eyes from the slender sun-polished legs. Ellen's hair blew in the wind, and he noticed a faint sprinkle of freckles across the bridge of her nose.

"When you've stared as long as necessary," she said without turning her head, "you can tell me why you wanted to talk to me."

Darrell grinned. Ellen was not in her friendliest mood. "You're the only one in the family who *will* talk. I'm staring at you because every time I see you, you look prettier."

Ellen made a scornful sound.

"Let's go somewhere and have lunch," Darrell suggested.

"No, thank you."

"Aren't you hungry? It's after one."

"You can eat if you like. I'll wait in the car."

"At least we can have a drink somewhere."

She nodded distantly, swung downhill toward the water-front.

"What about that truck? Or lorry, rather?" Darrell asked.

"It was light gray with a dump bed. Rather a large lorry."

"Large light-gray dump-truck," said Darrell. "Anything peculiar or noticeable characteristics that might attract attention?"

"Of course not," said Ellen. "What kind of a fool do you take Arthur for?"

"No fool whatever. It was just a forlorn hope."

"I suppose you have something ingenious in mind?"

"I want to ask at service stations where Noel might have refueled."

"You'll get nowhere. There's hundreds of similar lorries on the road. They're used by the road-menders. That's why Arthur bought it, to deceive the French."

"I see." They swung out on the Avenida de España, drove to the right, paralleling the fine wide beach.

"How did you learn about Erfoud?" asked Ellen. "Arthur certainly never told you, nor Duff."

"Nor you."

"You never asked me."

"Would you have told me?"

"Certainly. Why not?"

"I wish I'd asked you. I got my information the hard way. From a Moroccan, Moulay something ben Jilali. Do you know him?"

"I've heard the name. He's contact in Fez for the Algerian rebels — bigwig politician of some kind."

"Do you know Abd Allah el Kazim?"

"No. Who is he?"

"In the same line of business. Not a friendly chap. He insists that Noel killed his brother."

Ellen laughed in great good humor. "If he's an old-fashioned Moslem he'll want to kill you."

"You seem pleased."

"I'd like to see cemeteries full of Hutsons." But there was more gloom than sting in her voice. She stamped suddenly down on the accelerator, as if surprised to find herself driving at so modest a speed. The road ahead was comparatively clear; Darrell held his tongue.

"Where did you meet these Moroccans?" Ellen asked presently.

"They met me. They knew I had a letter from Noel. Slip-Slip apparently told them; he heard me talking to Duff the first day I arrived."

Ellen nodded. "Slip-Slip's been watching the docks — just in case Noel should try to cut out for Spain. I'd hate to be in Noel's shoes when they catch him." She turned Darrell a quick malicious side-glance. "You'll be in hot water too, if anyone decides for certain that you and Noel are working together."

"The idea's ridiculous."

"Not so ridiculous. It's occurred to everyone."

She swung into the parking area of a shore-side restaurant, ran a comb through her wind-blown hair, jumped to the ground. Darrell followed her across the parking area, out on a terrace overlooking the sea, to a table under a large orange and green parasol. Ellen flung herself into a chair, insolently crossed her legs, exchanged stares with the other patrons.

A waiter came, Darrell ordered. Ellen watched him with sardonic disinterest. "Does Arthur realize that you plan to go to Erfoud?"

"I haven't told him."

"I advise you not to. He doesn't approve of your investigation."

"He's unreasonable."

"You forget that Arthur is very upset. He put his money on a sure thing, but instead he finds himself destitute. I and Duff likewise, of course. The house is up for sale; we're to be out by the end of the week. The car is mine only until that odious Mr. Burdette catches me. The *Deirdre* is gone, or will be in a few days."

Darrell looked uncomfortably out to sea. "Where are you moving to?" he asked.

"I don't know. I'm sick of Tangier, and everything else I can think of." The waiter brought the drinks, Ellen picked up her glass, tilted it, clinking the ice back and forth. "What will you do if you find the heroin? Not that it's likely."

"Throw the stuff in the ocean, I suppose. What would you do if you found it?"

She drank, set the glass down with airy nonchalance. "Sell it to Ventriss and clear out. Before Arthur did me in."

"You really believe Arthur would do you in?"

"I know he would, with pleasure. I'd kill him with even more."

"You're a savage little beast."

"I have my reasons. I suppose you're acquainted with *Hamlet*?"

"A few of us in the States have learned to read."

"Hmmf. Where did you go to school?"

"Massachusetts Institute of Technology."

"Is that one of your Ivy League colleges?"

"Hardly."

"Massachusetts is somewhere in the east, I believe. Or is it in the Bible Belt?"

Darrell understood that she was mocking him. "Since you're leaving Tangier, you should visit the States and see for yourself."

"A hundred eighty million Phil Beresfords? No, thanks. How are you going to Erfoud?"

"I'll rent a car."

"I'll drive you — for ten thousand francs. You'll have to buy the petrol."

Darrell looked at her in surprise. "It's a long way."

"I know where Erfoud is."

"We'd have to spend the night."

"Not necessarily together."

"Not necessarily. I presume there'd be a surcharge if we did."

"Since you'll be saving money on the car, you might be able to afford it."

"Not at a hundred and forty dollars — or whatever your price is. But I've no objection if you want to drive me, purely as a business arrangement. Ten thousand francs and expenses. Correct?"

"Correct."

"One other matter which we had better settle now. If by some chance we find this heroin, I don't plan to turn it over to you."

Ellen's eyes glinted. "Perhaps you'll give me half. Half for me, half for you."

Darrell wondered if she were still mocking. "No. I won't give you half, or any."

"Qualms of morality?"

"Call it what you like. That much heroin can wreck a hundred lives. Perhaps a thousand, or ten thousand, for all I know."

"That's where you're wrong, my muddle-headed friend. The heroin wrecks no lives. The lives are already wrecked. The heroin is the symptom, not the cause. I'll tell you a secret, Mr. Hutson." She sat up, put her elbows on the table. "This is not the best of all possible worlds. In fact it's an evil world."

"It's just a world, neither good nor evil."

"Human beings are the world, and human beings live by evil. Evil is like air, so basic and pervading that you don't notice it."

"I can't admit that."

"No? Look. Look there on the street."

Darrell turned his head, to see a man in a dirty and ragged djellaba, a small overloaded donkey. The man carried a short sharp stick, which he repeatedly thrust into the donkey's haunch, with a twisting vicious pressure. Occasionally he made a target of an open sore. The donkey, dazed and dull, either refused or was unable to move more quickly, and only jerked his head.

"Look," said Ellen. "Look at these people around us. Are they excited or indignant? They pay no attention. You would not have looked either. You pretend the evil doesn't exist. The man tortures the donkey. The Russians torture the Hungarians. Americans torture Negroes. Evil is everywhere. You're so excited about the heroin; why don't you do something about the man who tortures his donkey?"

Darrell looked at her sullenly. "What could I do?"

"Jab him with his own stick. Explain that the donkey feels exactly the same sensation. You'd also have to buy the donkey, or the man would have his revenge later."

Darrell sat silently looking across the sea.

"Well," said Ellen gently. "You're not plunging to the donkey's rescue. Why not? You're afraid to make a scene. And you know that this one little viciousness is just a drop in an ocean of evil. Since you tolerate an active evil, you are passively evil, because by your intervention you could stop it. Presently you'll go home and resume your old life, selling sausages or whatever you do, and go along quite placidly. You'll buy a new car every year, complain at the price of ice cream and steak, you'll get fat and even more pompous, and continue to maintain that the world is sweet and good."

"Hey!" Darrell protested. "I'm not quite as bad as all that."

Ellen paid no attention to him. "I think I detest the passive evil more than the active evil. The Russians smothered the Hungarian rebellion. It was a vile act. All over the world people coughed and averted their eyes. Sometimes they called names like fox terriers barking from behind a fence. That nauseating Nehru denied that anything happened. There's a certain grandeur in the evil of the Russians. The people who look on are merely despicable."

Darrell recalled his visit to the house of Jilali in Fez. Without resistance he had submitted to search. A rational submission. Dishonorable? He did not know. Certainly it had been humiliating, and he burned at the recollection. He said, almost savagely, "I make compromises, I won't deny it. But I neither torture donkeys nor sell narcotics. And I don't recall that you ran out to protect that donkey."

"No. I admit I'm evil. I know it. I'm evil and callous and cowardly. I make no other pretense."

Darrell was surprised to see tears glistening in her eyes. He looked guiltily away.

For a space they sat in a not uncompanionable silence, sipping their drinks, looking across the bright water.

"Over-reaction," said Darrell in a meditative voice.

"What about it?"

"Just a thought. About you. Anyone so preoccupied with ethics can't be bad. You're much more virtuous and idealistic than I am."

Ellen rose to her feet. "First you make me listen to your platitudes, then you smear me all over with sentimentality. Furthermore, if we find that heroin — which I doubt — please don't attempt any gallant gestures on behalf of society."

"I'm not looking for heroin," said Darrell. "I'm looking for Noel. If just by chance I did locate the heroin, I plan to do something drastic to it. Arthur, Duff, the FLN, and yourself notwithstanding."

"Bah," sneered Ellen. "You and your windy heroics."

They returned to the car. Ellen said shortly, "We'd better start early. It's a long drive."

"You still want to go?"

"Certainly. Do you think your attitude surprises me?"

"I suppose not. Well, what time is early? Six o'clock? Eight o'clock?"

"About seven. I'll fill up with petrol tonight. You'll have to give me my money now, also five thousand francs for petrol."

"Good heavens," said Darrell, "are you that short?"

"Short? I'm broke. Why do you think I'm hiring out as a chauffeur?"

"I don't know. I don't want to take advantage of you. Ten thousand francs isn't very much, really. Maintenance, tires, depreciation — things like that —"

"Mr. Burdette's loss, not mine."

Darrell gave her fifteen thousand francs. "Seven o'clock in the morning, then."

✳

Late that evening Darrell wandered into the Masquerade for a nightcap. He bought Phil Beresford a drink and settled his debt.

T-Bone came in from the Balmoral lobby. At the sight of Darrell she stopped short, then turned and quickly went back through the glass and iron door.

"Duff doesn't need to worry about me," Darrell told Phil. "I'm far down T-Bone's list."

Phil was puzzled. "Because of breaking a dinner date? That's easy to fix. Just ask her again."

Darrell shook his head. "Yesterday in Fez I saw a photograph of Noel—a fake photograph. His face came from that picture with T-Bone on the beach."

"Odd," remarked Phil. "Odd indeed. And so?"

"Well, I happened to meet her this afternoon, down in the Place de France, and I asked her about it. Just idle curiosity—did she have a copy, had she lost one recently? Did she know this Abd Allah el Kazim? T-Bone denied everything with considerable indignation."

"The problem is solved," said Phil. "You tweaked her most mysterious secret. T-Bone's practicing to be an undercover agent."

Darrell was shocked. "Upshaw told me she carried tales to the French. She can't work for the Arabs at the same time?"

"It's just one of T-Bone's fantasies," said Phil. "Just now she considers herself a double agent. She'll take on as many customers as she can get. Why don't you set her after Noel? She'd ferret him out."

"If I don't make some headway pretty soon, I might do just that."

"Have you got any leads, if you don't mind my asking?"

"Nothing everybody else hasn't got. Tomorrow night at this time things might be different. I'm going out to where he disappeared."

Chapter XI

Darrell awoke at six o'clock to a call from the desk. For a moment he lay drowsily, collecting his thoughts. Today, Erfoud. Ellen McKinstry was coming by to pick him up. Darrell threw off the covers, swung out of bed.

He showered, shaved, dressed, descended to the lobby, where rolls and coffee awaited him. It was another miraculous spring day, with strands of golden sunlight sifting through the acacia branches.

At seven Darrell went out to stand in the street. Ten after seven, seven-fifteen. Then, preceded by the now-familiar throb, the Mercedes-Benz rounded the corner, slid up the hill.

Darrell stepped forward; the car stopped. Ellen looked out at him, face clear, mouth relaxed. Darrell found it hard to control a smile. Ellen's gaze narrowed. "What's funny?"

"Nothing whatever," Darrell apologized. "Just high spirits."

"Jump in before Arthur looks down from his window and sees us."

Darrell seated himself. "What if he does?"

"A good point. We're of one mind there." She shifted into low. "What if he does?" The car roared up the hill. "We're off and it's a beautiful day."

This time Darrell held a straight face. He swung around in the seat and looked her over. She wore her turtle-neck sweater, a gray tweed skirt, moccasins, a beret which more or less successfully constrained her hair. "Have you had breakfast?" Darrell asked.

"Just tea."

"Are you hungry?"

"No."

Conversation languished. The Mercedes-Benz found the open road. The speedometer needle swung up, across the dial. Then they met a patch of heavier traffic — trucks, a bus packed full with white-robed passengers — and were forced to slacken speed.

"We don't go to Fez today," said Darrell.

"No. Straight on through from Meknes."

"I was in Fez two days ago, to see this Jilali person."

"Fools rush in, and so forth."

Darrell smiled faintly. "I had to get information somewhere."

"Did you enjoy Fez?" she asked politely.

"Not really. I was concerned with other matters. But the shops, or bazaars, whatever they're called —"

"The *souks*."

"They looked interesting, what I saw of them, which wasn't much."

Ellen thrust down on the accelerator; the Mercedes-Benz lunged ahead, around a truck. They pulled up behind a big yellow bus. Ellen swept around, avoiding an oncoming oil truck by half a second. Darrell glimpsed a startled face in the passing cab. Ahead a pair of camels walked beside the road. One of them turned its neck out, started to amble across to the other side. Ellen swerved; they passed under its neck. The mournful eyes looked down at Darrell.

"Ellen," said Darrell, "Ellen!"

"Yes?"

"Slow down, please."

"Too bad you're so nervy; we'd get there sooner."

"We've got all day."

"Now that we've shaken off the car that was following us."

Darrell whirled in the seat. The road was clear. He turned slowly back.

There was another period of silence. Ellen relaxed. In the rush of wind Darrell could not be sure, but it seemed as if Ellen were humming to herself.

Darrell kept watch on the road behind, but saw nothing suspicious. Finally he asked, "Was there really a car following us?"

"It left Tangier the same time we did, and stayed about the same distance behind; an old Renault or Fiat, something of the sort."

"Who would be interested in where we're going?"

She looked at him incredulously. "You can't be that naïve. You're Arthur's only hope. He's sure you're in touch with Noel. The Moroccans probably have the same idea. You're the focus of many eyes."

"That's ridiculous."

"Four hundred thousand pounds isn't ridiculous."

Darrell looked over his shoulder at the road behind. He saw a faint swirl of dust, retreating ranks of eucalyptus trees, a truck moving toward Tangier, with speed exaggerated by their own motion. He turned back. "I don't care much for this sort of adventure."

"You should have made this clear to your brother."

"I've made things clear to Noel from the first minute he could understand me. The more I talked, the worse he got. Two years ago I stopped talking."

"You have a sister too?"

"Yes. She's about your age."

"Undoubtedly much nicer than I am."

"In some ways. She's not as pretty as you are."

Her face became disdainful. "Pretty. What an insipid word."

"Handsome. Lovely. Attractive. Beautiful. Striking. Magnificent. Exquisite."

"Sex-mad, like all Americans."

Darrell said no more, but gave his attention to the passing landscape: groves of hag-ridden cork-oaks, dusty vineyards, rocky hillocks clumped with rosemary, spurge, asphodel.

Miles slid past, up hill, down dale; the Mercedes-Benz coursing as smooth as the electricity in the wires beside the road. The sun mounted, glaring white in the dusty blue sky.

At eleven they entered Meknes, where they stopped to refuel. Together they put the top up against the combined brilliance of sun and sky. Darrell offered to drive; Ellen curtly refused.

Studying the willful profile, Darrell wondered what went on behind the wind-blown thatch of hair.

They departed Meknes through the French town, seeing nothing of the old city except a glimpse of great mud ramparts to the north.

Ahead rose the Middle Atlas. The road became narrow, dusty, high-crowned, the sort of road which anywhere in the world leads to the back of beyond. Sun-burned foothills rose on either side, crusted with olive trees frangible as dry foam. The traffic became more various, more primitive: camels lurching and swaying; donkey caravans bringing shredded bark, hides and faggots out of the hills; goats herded by Berber women dressed in orange and lavender and black.

The road swung up the valleys, across the round ridges. The olive groves fell below, fresher, brighter vegetation appeared beside the road. The air became cool, sliding in a silent wind down the ravines. They came out on an upland savannah, open to the sky, with the mass of the mountains ahead, spattered with forest, streaked with snow.

At noon they came to Azrou, a lonely little French settlement. A Berber village of adobe houses occupied a nearby hillside: ten thousand rectangular shapes and shadows, a cubist construction painted in colors ground from sand, mud and lamp-black. Darrell suggested lunch; Ellen agreed without enthusiasm. She parked the car and alighted with the air of one reluctantly conferring a favor.

They ate in the dining room of a small French hotel. Ellen had nothing to say, and Darrell reminded himself that her moody preoccupation, whatever its cause, was no concern of his. The meal proceeded in silence and at last came to an end. Darrell called for the check; Ellen, opening her purse, brought out a thousand francs, which she tossed across the table. "What's this for?" asked Darrell.

"My lunch, obviously."

"Just as you like," said Darrell. "However, the arrangement was that I should pay expenses."

"Ostentation is not an endearing trait, Mr. Hutson."

"But, confound it, I'm not being ostentatious! I'm only —" Darrell stopped short. He took the money, and after paying the bill, returned her change.

They left the hotel. "Would you like me to drive?" asked Darrell with elaborate politeness.

"No, thank you." Ellen serenely seated herself behind the wheel. "I'm all on edge when anyone else drives." She started the motor, shifted into low. The Mercedes-Benz sprang down the road. Telephone poles began to snap to the rear.

Darrell said patiently, "You couldn't be as exasperating as this by accident. You must have a good reason for wanting me to hate you."

"None whatever. Haven't you discovered? I'm perverse."

"You'll discover yourself walking unless you slow down."

Ellen curled her lips in lofty contempt. "We won't reach Erfoud before evening."

"At least we'll get there."

The road began to climb, twisting, turning, bending back on itself in tight hairpins. Stands of cedar trees appeared; patches of snow lay in the shade. Half an hour after leaving Azrou they breasted up onto a high plateau. Snow lay deep to either side of the road, distorted black peaks jutted up on all sides.

Ellen glanced sidewise toward Darrell. "Unless you prefer to sit there glowering, I'll let you drive."

"I'll be glad to drive, if you want a rest."

Ellen considered. Darrell watched her frowning and debating and was rather surprised when without a word she stopped the car. They both jumped out, both circled the car. Meeting at the front, they almost bumped into each other. Darrell put his hands on her shoulders; they stared into each other's face. Ellen raised her eyebrows in frosty inquiry; slowly with great dignity she shook Darrell's hands from her shoulders. Raging inwardly, Darrell seated himself behind the wheel. Ellen picked a small white crocus growing beside the road, which she brought into the car with her.

Darrell told himself, she's either a lunatic, or a great actress. Distinctly a puzzling creature…If she wants me to hate her, she's not succeeding. The more I hate her, the more I want to kiss her. That's out, naturally. I wouldn't take advantage of her…So reflecting he adjusted the seat, gingerly shifted into low.

"Be careful not to oversteer," said Ellen. "When you turn the wheel, the car turns too."

Darrell touched the accelerator; the car slipped forward.

"You can do a hundred and forty on the flat," said Ellen. "Please don't try here."

After a few miles Darrell gained confidence. Ellen relaxed, curling sideways on the seat. Darrell once again felt a near-irresistible impulse to smile. He was certain his face did not move, but Ellen looked at him sharply. "Are you laughing at me?"

Darrell shook his head. "It's the wrong frame of mind for this particular project."

"Are you very fond of Noel?" asked Ellen.

Darrell shrugged. "We've never been close. He thinks I'm dull, I think he's foolish."

"Foolish? You're over-generous. Noel's an ass. Bumptious, noisy, bustling here and there, bursting with over-enthusiastic boyishness."

"Noel, like yourself, is a romantic."

"I romantic?" cried Ellen in astonishment. "What rot."

"Certainly you're a romantic."

She shook her tawny head. "Definitely not. Romanticism is a rosy veil across the eyes."

"The veil isn't necessarily rose-colored. But it exists."

"Aren't you being rather presumptuous?" said Ellen haughtily.

"Everyone has a right to his opinions. As a matter of fact, when I first met you I thought you were half-mad."

Ellen smiled with grim satisfaction. "And now?"

"I wouldn't like to say. You'd be annoyed and call me names."

"Perhaps. But tell me anyway."

"Well, there're three sections. First, you're a precocious brat."

"Hmm."

"Secondly, you're a romantic. You don't belong to this age. Where you do fit, I'm sure I don't know. Thirdly — I can't put it into words very clearly."

"Try."

"No. And this time I'll be firm."

They drove on in silence, across a rock-strewn moonscape, through a quiet winter-dull Berber town, Midelt, then entered a great down-slanting gap that yawned forward a vast distance, finally spreading apart into empty air. The snow vanished, the rocks were harsh and bare. They passed a half-dozen Berber villages: cubicles of mud and stone built wall to wall. The inhabitants watched them without animation; the men somber and weather-beaten, the women rather more spirited, in black-, white- and blue-striped robes, faces tattooed with blue designs.

They came to another town, Rich, with a French hotel, a few French shops, and now the Atlas lay behind. Ahead, still invisible behind a dwindling series of lesser hills, lay the Sahara.

Shortly after Rich they saw the first palms. The road now followed the Oued Ziz, a gray-green river, sluggish and shallow, with little cultivated plots along the banks. The palms began to appear in greater numbers, in clumps of two or three, then by the sixes and tens, then in a continuous green ribbon along the river.

With the sun hanging in the west they came to tomato-red Ksar-es-Souk, where they filled up with gas at a large modern service station. At Ksar-es-Souk the road divided. The principal fork led southwest, behind the Atlas, linking the kasbahs, or fortress villages, of the desert's edge to Ouarzazate and Marrakech. The lesser fork continued south to Erfoud and out in the desert to Taouz, this latter a caravan terminus.

Turning south to Erfoud, they passed a Land Rover parked beside the road. Four soldiers stood drinking coffee in tin cups from a Thermos on the fender. Ellen looked back over her shoulder. "French road patrol."

"Is there any chance the French captured Noel?"

"Very slight. The Moroccans would be sure to know."

The road now stretched across a dead desolation covered with innumerable millions of round black stones. In the distance a dark spot appeared, trailing dust like a comet. It grew, approached, passed: a big blue bus packed to capacity with crates, suitcases, bicycles, furniture, sacks and bundles. The dust settled slowly; again there was nothing to be seen but desert, flat as a griddle out to a far pair of cinnamon-colored buttes.

But the flatness was an illusion; suddenly the road dipped, slanted abruptly through bluffs of red sandstone, into the valley of the Ziz. Now the palms were more beautiful than ever; feathery and soft-looking, of various heights and various suave greens, leaning over gardens of fruit and grass and vegetables. The river swung wide to the right; the road climbed back to the desert floor, the fertile ribbon disappeared from view.

Kilometers passed, the sun hung low; the time was almost six o'clock. "Further than I had expected," Darrell remarked.

"Seven hundred kilometers," said Ellen colorlessly.

As the sun was sinking they came to a heavy crenelated wall among the palms: Erfoud. A side road turned off to the right, with a sign indicating the Gîte d'Etape. Darrell stopped the car. "Is that the hotel where Noel stayed?"

"So I understand."

"Unless you have objections we'll spend the night here."

"No objections whatever. This is your venture, not mine."

"Very well. I suppose they'll be able to feed us and give us beds."

"I imagine so."

The driveway wound through the palms; the Gîte d'Etape appeared silhouetted on the sunset. "Good heavens," said Darrell. "A hotel or a castle?"

"It's a hotel, waiting for tourists which so far haven't arrived."

"And this is where Noel telephoned to Tangier?"

"Yes."

"And when he left here —"

"He disappeared."

The road curved up, ended in a graveled parking area. Darrell switched off the ignition, opened the door for Ellen, followed her out. He looked around the landscape. "What a beautiful spot."

"Very romantic."

Darrell took her arm. "I refuse to be enemies with you. We'll wash up; we'll have a drink and dinner and pretend that we're friends."

"You're paying the piper, you can call the tune." She pulled her arm free. "But I don't care to dance."

A page pushed open plate-glass doors; they climbed carpeted steps to the great bright lobby.

Darrell went to the registration desk. The clerk, a man thin and precise, wearing horn-rimmed glasses, bowed. He showed no surprise when Darrell requested two rooms.

"If you will leave your passports, please." He spoke English with only a trace of accent. "Do you wish dinner?"

"Later in the evening."

"And your car, you wish it garaged?"

"Please."

The page conducted them to their rooms, which gave on a balcony circling the lobby. Darrell said to Ellen, "After I wash up, I'm going down to talk to the clerk. So I'll meet you in the lobby."

"Do you prefer to talk to the clerk alone?" asked Ellen in her most colorless voice.

"Not at all. If you like, I'll wait for you."

"I won't be long."

When Darrell came down the stairs, Ellen sat perched on the arm of a chair. In deep leather chairs nearby sat a middle-aged couple, the only other guests visible.

"Would you like a drink first?" Darrell asked.

"Whatever you please."

"It might help with the inquiry."

They crossed the lobby to the bar. Darrell ordered highballs, then looked around the lobby. "One month ago Noel sat here. He'd just killed a man — el Kazim's brother. Undoubtedly he came to the bar, undoubtedly he had a few drinks." He looked speculatively at the bartender, who, he had discovered while ordering the highballs, spoke only French. "Ask him if he remembers Noel."

Ellen spoke in French. The bartender listened, appeared to think, replied.

"He remembers Noel," said Ellen, "but did not talk to him. Noel had three or four drinks, he thinks."

"Does he remember anything else?"

The answer was an uninterested *"Non, madame."*

"Not too illuminating," said Darrell. "Well, shall we tackle the clerk?"

"Whenever you're ready."

They crossed the lobby. The clerk put his hands correctly and precisely on the plate glass. "Yes, sir?"

"My name is Darrell Hutson, as you already know."

"Yes, sir."

"A month ago my brother stayed here. Noel Hutson."

"Yes. I remember. Other gentlemen have made inquiries. I hope there is no trouble."

"None, except that I haven't been able to find him."

The clerk shook his head. "I'm sorry to hear that, sir. But I know nothing. He left no address."

"It is very puzzling," said Darrell. "I understand that he telephoned to Tangier?"

"Yes. I've discussed this with the other gentlemen. He telephoned to Tangier, and left a message for a man named Arthur. I could not help overhearing, and of course I have been asked several times about it."

"Do you remember the message?"

"Not distinctly. I paid no attention after Mr. Hutson finally reached his party. It was something like, 'Send somebody down here. I do not care to drive to Tangier with this load.' And then he said, 'Yes, at the Gîte.' I don't think he said much more."

"He asked only for Arthur? No one else?"

"In the second call I believe he did mention another person."

"Duff?"

"Yes, Duff. That is the name. But he left the message to be given to Arthur."

Darrell turned to Ellen. "Arthur never got the message?"

"He says not."

"I don't suppose you answered the phone."

"No," said Ellen. "It was not I. Arthur's mind has been exploring the same channels. It wasn't Aktouf, so it must be I. But I wasn't home."

Darrell rubbed his chin. "There was something else I wanted to ask. Oh yes." He turned to the clerk. "You said he *finally* reached his party. He made more than one call?"

"Two calls. He failed to reach his party on the first call. And on the second call he left the message."

Darrell ran his fingers through his hair. He looked at Ellen dubiously. "Strange."

"Why strange?"

"He made two calls. It stands to reason that he would first have called the Balmoral. Then he would have tried your house, where he might have expected to find Duff if Upshaw weren't there."

"Very well, I agree to that. As does everyone else."

"But on Noel's first call he made no connection. So he must have called your house first, and then the hotel. But this doesn't make sense, for two reasons. Because he asked for Duff and because Aktouf never took the message — so I've been assured." He turned back to the clerk. "These were the only calls he made? Just these two?"

"Two are all he made, sir. I have told the other gentlemen the same."

"I suppose you're sure of this?"

"Yes, sir. He came down from his room and made only two calls. It will be evident from his bill." He opened a drawer, flipped back through a sparse set of papers, withdrew a statement. "Two calls, as I have —" He peered. "No, there are three." He looked up in puzzlement. "But I am sure he called only twice. Perhaps he used his room telephone while I was at my dinner. That, of course, is possible. The manager would have made the connection." He looked at Darrell in concern. "Is this an important matter? I told the other gentlemen —"

"It's of no significance," said Darrell. "The numbers are not noted on his bill?"

"No, sir."

"I see. And the other gentlemen who asked are not aware that Mr. Hutson made three calls?"

"No, sir."

"These three were the only calls he made?"

"They are all. Of course he received a call in the morning."

"So I understand. Were you on duty?"

The clerk nodded with a kind of terse pride. "We do not have many guests, and consequently a minimum staff. I am on duty mornings and evenings. The manager relieves me during the afternoon and during my meals."

"Do you remember what time Mr. Hutson left?"

"I think about seven o'clock. He took no breakfast, as I recall."

"And what time did the call come through?"

"I don't remember exactly, sir. Just after Mr. Hutson had left."

"Did the person who called identify himself?"

"No, sir."

"I assume it was a man who called?" From the corner of his eye Darrell saw Ellen stiffen.

"I believe so, sir. I hardly remember."

"There was no message?"

"No."

"Is there anything else you remember about Noel? Any detail? Did he speak to anyone?"

"No, sir. We had no other guests that night. In fact, Mr. Hutson was our only guest during four days." He smiled. "It makes it easier to remember when there are so few guests. He posted a letter, of course."

"Did you notice the address?"

"A letter to the United States, I believe."

"Anything else?"

"That's all I remember, sir."

"Did anyone else speak to him? The manager?"

"I don't believe so. The other gentlemen inquired, but I am sure the manager told them nothing."

Darrell looked at Ellen. "Can you think of anything to ask?"

"No."

Darrell turned back to the clerk. "May we speak to the manager?"

"He is not here, sir. He is at a conference in Casablanca."

"Oh, I see. Thanks very much for your help." He laid a thousand francs on the counter.

"Thank you, sir."

Darrell took Ellen's arm, led her back toward the bar. Half-way across the lobby she became conscious of his grasp, and disengaged herself.

"Young hellion," said Darrell mildly.

"I hired out to drive you. If you want to exercise your gallantry, you'll have to pay more."

"I'll keep to myself. I know your rates."

"They've gone up. I've decided you're a bore."

With exaggerated formality Darrell seated her in one of the deep leather chairs, ordered another round of highballs from the bar.

"Do you know anything now you didn't know before?" asked Ellen in her coolest and most flippant manner.

"I know that Noel made three telephone calls instead of two."

"Is that significant? He never did speak to Arthur, and the message never was delivered."

"So Arthur claims."

"You don't believe him?"

"Arthur could be playing a deep game."

Ellen shook her head. "Not that deep. Noel made three calls instead of two. What else?"

"The telephone call in the morning came after Noel had left."

"Is that all?"

"That's all."

"It seems to me you've had your trouble for nothing."

"Perhaps. We're not finished yet."

"No?"

"The call that came in the morning intrigues me. Who called him? Certainly no girl friend."

"What difference does it make? Noel was already on his way."

"Why should anyone call him? Who knew he was here?"

"It's immaterial. He'd already decided to scuttle. He was well on his way to Casablanca."

Darrell shook his head. "If that's what he intended, why bother to call Arthur?"

Ellen looked at him, her lip curling in impatience. "Because he changed his mind! Because four hundred thousand pounds is a great deal of money to think about all night!"

"I know Noel better than that. He might talk himself into delivering a load of guns, but Noel wouldn't touch narcotics. It would violate his whole picture of himself, destroy his self-respect. He was probably more concerned with how to get rid of the stuff."

Ellen snorted. "In that case, why not fling it in the ditch?"

"Perhaps out of loyalty to Arthur, even though he despised the whole business."

"What rot."

"Not at all. He'd feel bound to declare himself. That's exactly what he did. He says so in his letter to me. Although I still don't understand what he meant by coppering his bets —"

"Coppering his bets?"

Darrell reached in his pocket. "You haven't seen the letter."

Ellen read it with interest. "It doesn't sound as if Noel planned to decamp. Still, he might have changed his mind."

"Barely possible. But 'coppering his bets'— how? He must have had the FLN in mind. If they learned that he had killed el Kazim's brother, he'd get short shrift. He wanted to make sure of reaching Tangier, or Casablanca — wherever he was headed for. Shall we have dinner?"

"If you like."

Darrell rose to his feet, held out his hand. She ignored it, jumped up, sauntered ahead of him to the dining room.

The head waiter, wearing tails and a glistening shirt, ushered them across the echoing dining room. Fifty tables glittered with silver and sparkled with crystal under three massive chandeliers. Darrell and Ellen were seated beside one of the tall plate-glass windows overlooking the palm grove. Across the room the elderly couple were already eating, attended by two waiters. The dining room otherwise was empty.

Hors d'oeuvres were served, wine was uncorked and poured. An enormous apricot moon rose behind the far pinnacles. Darrell thought, if I make a comment Ellen will sneer about American sentimentalism; hence I'll say nothing. He pretended to ignore the moon and from the corner of his eye watched Ellen. She looked at the moon, turned him a searching glance, then looked back across the moonlit palm grove.

Darrell could contain himself no longer. "Even if we don't find Noel, I'm glad I came."

"It's pleasant here," Ellen agreed grudgingly.

"You've never been here before?"

"Is this your idea of how to grill a suspect?"

"An idle question, pure and simple."

"I've never been to Erfoud before."

They ate in silence. The elderly couple finished, rose and stalked from the room. The moon floated high over the hills, the palm grove was like a growth of dark crystals.

Dinner came to an end. Darrell and Ellen returned to the lobby, where they stood uncertainly, neither meeting the other's eyes.

"Would you like to go for a walk?"

"A walk in the moonlight?" said Ellen indifferently. "All right, if you like."

The page ran ahead to open the plate-glass doors; they wandered out into the wan white glare. The palm grove lay before them, black net and cloth-of-silver; they turned off along a path. The moonlight illuminated the landscape to the finest detail; each clod of earth threw an India-ink shadow; each lead-foil blade of grass, each platinum cat-whisker maintained a fragile distinction from every other. From the direction of the kasbah came the sounds of life: the barking of a dog, frogs croaking, the dry whistle of crickets.

They wandered on: Darrell took Ellen's hand; after ten seconds she snatched it away. "Excuse me," said Darrell with dignity.

They came to an open area, spiked here and there with two-foot stones. "A graveyard," said Ellen. "They just dig down a few feet, put in the body, cover it with a stone at the head and feet."

They turned back into the grove. Darrell said, "I've been very annoyed with Noel, but if it hadn't been for his letter I'd never be here. Your company is at least stimulating... I'm beginning to fear the worst."

"About what?"

"About Noel. If he were alive —"

"Noel, Noel, Noel," said Ellen crossly. "Is that all you think about?"

Darrell heaved a deep sigh. "You're a complete puzzle. When I take your hand, you vault away as if I were a leper. When I'm properly respectful, you find fault again."

Ellen stooped, picked a blade of grass. "Yes," she said thoughtfully. "I'm inconsistent and perverse..." She faced him, put her hands on his shoulders. "Kiss me."

"Free?"

"Yes. Free."

Darrell kissed her... A peculiar kiss, he realized with the disengaged fraction of his mind: warm, pliant, earnest — but somewhere behind lay another quality, cool careful attention. Darrell kissed her forehead. Ellen stood quietly. Darrell looked down into her face. Am I insane? Am I imagining things? Why is she watching so closely? Does she want me to make love to her? Is she teasing, blowing hot and cold?... He relaxed his grip. Ellen and her motives were beyond his understanding.

She stood soberly looking up at the moon. Her mouth relaxed, her eyes were clear; she looked young and innocent and full of dreams. Darrell once again put her into the context of his life at home. He saw her frying eggs at a counter-top stove, sprawled out reading the Sunday newspapers, excitedly planning a new house... Good heavens, thought Darrell, where are my thoughts taking me?

"What are you thinking?" she asked.

Darrell focused on her face. She was watching him intently. He took her hands; they lay warm, subtly responsive in his. "I was thinking of you, naturally."

"What kind of thoughts?"

Darrell shook his head. "I'm confused, like a neurotic rat in a laboratory. I don't know which button to push. You hate me and despise me, and then when I kiss you it's like a mixture of whiskey and electricity."

She started to speak, then caught herself. "Kiss me."

"No," said Darrell sadly. "Much as I'd like to."

"Are you afraid?"

"No…Yes…This is like hitting myself with a hammer…I made an arrangement with you. I've already violated the spirit of it. By kissing you."

"But I asked you to. That releases you from the agreement." Ellen's voice was soft as the moonlight, silky and wan.

"That's true — in a way. It releases me from my agreement with you, but not from my agreement with me. It's not that I don't want to. But something tells me, no, Darrell. Don't cave in so easily. I don't know why…Good lord," he said in disgust. "How I'm babbling."

Ellen picked another blade of grass, chewed on it. "Very revealing."

He picked a blade of grass for himself. "It's not that I'm not willing. When we get back to Tangier, we'll go somewhere — come back here if you like — and stay a week. Do you like that idea?"

"Whether I do or not, now is now, and now is different."

"That's exactly the trouble! Now is different! I made that damned bargain. It's a contract and I can't quit just because the going gets rough. You wouldn't want me to."

"But I do."

Darrell put his hands on her shoulders, looked into her moonlit face. "You want me to break this contract made with you and with myself?" Suddenly it seemed he was approaching some glimmer of understanding, some hint — vague, fragmentary — of the truth. It was bigger than he ever had imagined.

"Yes, if you like."

Darrell stared at her eyes; some trick of the moonlight gave them a weird shine; her mouth smiled at a strange angle.

"But I won't do it, naturally." He dropped his hands, turned away. Astonishing. Five minutes before he had been thinking fatuous thoughts about this girl, picturing her as a part of his life. Now they were separated by a gulf far darker than the distance to the moon.

She asked in a measured voice, "Why are you looking at me like that?"

"I'm trying to understand you."

"Are you succeeding?"

"I'm groping. It's hard going. I'm not used to these situations."

"What have you arrived at so far?"

"You encouraged me to lose my head, to break my promise — in short to make a fool of myself."

"Why yes. So I did."

"I understand that — but why?"

"I have my reasons." She spoke airily, but she turned her head away, switched at her leg with the blade of grass.

"Are they secret?"

"Yes. But I'll tell you." She threw down the blade of grass. "Perhaps you wonder why I came out here like this, put myself in this position."

"Not after we made our arrangement."

She made an angry gesture. "I came out here because I wanted to hate you. I've been anxious for a chance to hate you. You haven't given me any opportunity. You've frustrated everything. And I hate you for that!"

Darrell said in an astonished voice, "But why? Why do you want to hate me?"

"I hate all men," said Ellen. "I hate men like poison." She turned and walked rapidly back toward the hotel.

Darrell seated himself on the bank of a convenient irrigation ditch. Ellen. He spoke the name aloud, hoping that some inner reflex would give him a clue to his emotions. His subconscious was no help.

He rose to his feet, returned to the hotel. The lobby was bare of guests. Ellen had gone to her room. Darrell sat at the bar, ordered a highball, drank it; ordered another, took it to one of the deep leather chairs.

The dining room was dark, the clerk stood idly behind the desk, the bartender read a magazine. Darrell studied the Berber rugs. He counted them; there were seventeen. The patterns were barbaric, the colors even more so, dissonance which sophisticated minds would never think to employ: ocher with salmon pink; lavender, saffron and peacock blue; black, white, lemon yellow, pumpkin orange…A step. Ellen, pale but composed, seated herself beside him. "May I have a drink?"

"Immediately." He ordered a highball for her and another for himself.

She leaned back, scrutinized him impassively. Darrell returned the inspection, trying to recapture the insight he had felt in the palm grove: not to reinforce the unpleasant impression, but to prove or disprove its validity. No avail. Ellen was a composed if pale young woman with a sullen reckless expression. Darrell finished his second highball, started on his third. He was tired and unsettled; the Scotch had a soothing effect. Ellen made short work of her own highball. "Another?" asked Darrell. She nodded; Darrell signaled the bartender.

He thrust his legs out, leaned back in the chair. "Something I'm not clear on. You hate men — all men. May I ask why?"

"Yes, you may ask," said Ellen, "and I'll tell you. It's something I've only told one other person, and he's dead." She took a long sip of her highball, continued in a flat voice: "When I was younger — fourteen, to be exact — I had a very unpleasant experience."

"Oh?"

"Yes. Through the instrumentality of — let us say — a close acquaintance."

Darrell could think of nothing to say.

"I told my father. He was furious. The same night he was killed."

There was a period of silence. Darrell fought to subdue a sense of unreality. "You don't mean — Arthur."

"I mean Arthur."

"But you're his niece."

"You and your fat round little set of rules! What difference does that make? He's a man!"

Darrell paused to collect his wits. "Then you think that your father spoke to him, that they had an argument, a fight, and Arthur shot your father."

"I'm sure of it. I've planned to kill Arthur ever since. I've tried at least twenty times. I can't do it. I went so far as to point a gun at him once. I couldn't pull the trigger."

"Does Arthur know this?"

"Of course he knows."

"Does Duff know?"

"Duff? He doesn't care."

Darrell reached out for her hand. She jerked violently away. "Don't touch me."

"I'm only trying to console you. Clumsily, no doubt."

"I don't want your sympathy. I don't need it."

"Certainly you do. Why brood? You're young —"

"I'm old and wise and evil as a witch."

They sat in silence. "Another highball?" Darrell asked.

"All right."

Darrell signaled for another round, his head already a trifle light. "We'll both be drunk in another ten minutes."

"Afraid?" asked Ellen.

Darrell shook his head. "No. But returning to this hate business: you hate Arthur, well and good. Why herd me in with him? This project of yours — coming down here to hate me — is it quite fair?"

Ellen said in an uninterested voice, "I warned you that I was unmoral."

"I didn't believe you. I still don't."

"I've tried to prove it to you."

Darrell shook his head. "You can't deny that you're honest. I haven't suspected you of lying to me."

"Please, Mr. Hutson, don't inflict me with a code of morals I've insisted on denying. Besides," she added irrelevantly, "you're hardly the one to preach of fairness."

"So?" Darrell was surprised and disturbed. "I'm not conscious of unfairness."

"Because you're a stupid egotist, much like Duff."

Darrell winced, grinning ruefully. "Explain."

"You make me a magnanimous offer — a sordid week in a hotel. Do you expect me to clap my hands in excitement?"

Darrell fidgeted with his highball. "It does sound sordid now. Then it didn't."

Ellen snorted. "You preen yourself on your faithfulness to the terms of a contract. Integrity? Dedication? No. You're afraid to break your so-called arrangement. You're a moral weakling. You don't have the courage to adapt to a changed situation. You're afraid of guilt. It's not the act itself you want to avoid — in fact you hopefully propose a week of the same — but only after you break the taboo by touching home base at Tangier. Isn't that the act of a prig?"

Darrell listened in wry discomfort. "Well, you've done it."

"Done what?"

"You've figured out a way to hate me. And you couldn't rest till you came down to tell me about it."

Ellen sat bolt upright, stiff as the back of a chair. Then she relaxed, fell limply back. "Very well. And I've told you."

"You certainly have. There's enough truth in what you say to make me hate myself. I'm afraid of guilt. I admit it. Fear of guilt is a poor guide to the conduct of one's life. Better than none, of course. Well — that's that. You hate me; I'm disillusioned with you and myself both. The pattern of our relationship is set. Which is for the best. When I leave Tangier there'll be no pangs for either of us."

Ellen stood up. "None whatever. I'm going to bed."

"Good night."

She made no answer. He watched the slender figure crossing the lobby, the jaunty stride now just a trifle listless.

Darrell sat with his head whirling, feeling the alcohol with his body, thinking with a mind which had never seemed more clear. He looked at himself from a dispassionate height. Ellen was bitingly right. He had prided himself on his conservatism; he was no more than a coward. He had conducted himself according to precepts, and found that he set greater store by the precepts than by the honor they represented. He yearned for Ellen, but feared to venture anything for her. He had pictured a week in a hotel room but had blocked out of his mind the larger vision. She had a right to despise him. The problem suggested its own solution. He made a decision. So much for that.

There was Noel to consider. But where was the problem? The

situation seemed crystal-clear. Astonishing, that he should have felt a momentary puzzlement! Arthur Upshaw, the Moroccans — were they so stupid, so dense? But no. He did them an injustice. They were ignorant of two key facts. First, Noel would never use a shipment of heroin for his own financial gain. Second, there had been three telephone calls instead of two.

Darrell rose unsteadily to his feet. The clerk had departed, the lobby was almost dark. Darrell nodded good night to the bartender, who put down his magazine with relief.

Darrell went up to his room, removed his clothes. The hotel was silent. Through the open window came the sound of frogs and crickets. He thought of Ellen, only a few feet down the hall, listening to the same sounds. He wanted to go to her, to tell her everything: of his decisions, his deductions, the probable whereabouts of Noel. But his head was swimming; he felt limp and wrung dry of energy. She would misunderstand; it would be a mess. Darrell heaved a sigh, composed himself to sleep.

Chapter XII

EARLY SUNLIGHT STREAMING THROUGH the window aroused Darrell. Half-awake he raised his arm, focused on his watch. Seven o'clock.

After a few minutes he propped himself up, threw his legs over the side of the bed. His head felt thick. He staggered into the bathroom. There was no hot water. Cursing and hissing between clenched teeth, he stepped under the cold shower.

Fifteen minutes later he was shaved and dressed, ready for the day. He went to Ellen's door, knocked. There was no response.

He knocked again. Still no answer.

Darrell descended the stairs. The lobby was dim and empty, the dining room locked. He went to the front door, looked out over the parking area. No sign of Ellen. Darrell stood deep in reflection. At the far wall a glass door opened out upon a balcony. Darrell crossed the lobby with swift steps. Ellen stood by the rail, looking thoughtfully over the bright landscape.

Darrell joined her. "Good morning."

"Good morning." Ellen looked fresh and crisp.

"I pounded on your door. When you didn't answer I thought you'd left for home."

"It didn't occur to me."

Darrell leaned on the rail. The palm grove had no secrets in the morning sunlight; the previous evening seemed unreal.

"What do you intend to do today?" Ellen asked indifferently.

"Throw out a line for Noel. I have a theory I'd like to test; it came to me last night after you'd gone to bed."

Ellen glanced at him with aversion.

"Not immediately after you'd left, of course," said Darrell hurriedly. "I sat drinking and worrying and fretting, wondering about things. Then this idea about Noel came to me. I turned it over a few times, and there it was. I've figured the whole thing out."

"An exercise in pure reason?"

Darrell nodded. "It's not particularly difficult."

"Your theory can't be very sound. Arthur has been cudgeling his brain an entire month, and Arthur isn't stupid."

"Arthur has been working under two handicaps. The idea that Noel would refuse to steal a million dollars is beyond his imagination. Then he only knew of two calls to Tangier. The first presumably to your house, the second to the Balmoral. Since Aktouf took no message, Arthur wonders who did."

"He thinks it was the other way around. The first call to the Balmoral, the second to the house. He thinks I answered the phone and then never gave him the message."

"Well, either way it makes no difference. We know that Noel made three calls: the first from his room, almost surely to the hotel; the second to your house; the third, where? Someone answered, call him X. Noel gives X a message for Arthur, to the effect that if Arthur wants his heroin hauled, Arthur had better come to Erfoud and haul it himself."

"Yes. I follow you there."

"Noel sits here in the lobby, jumping at every sound. He's just killed a man, his nerves are in poor shape. There's no word from Arthur, so in the morning he leaves — about seven. A few minutes later someone telephones, asks for him. Who? Arthur?"

Ellen shook her head. "Arthur insists that he received no message from Noel."

"Probably not," said Darrell. "More likely Mr. X. Now think. Noel called Tangier at seven or eight o'clock in the evening. The call came the next morning at about seven-thirty. A lapse of approximately twelve hours. Right?"

"Right."

"We left Tangier yesterday at seven-thirty in the morning; we drove at a fairly good pace, arrived here at seven. A lapse of eleven and a half hours. Very close to the same interval."

"Right again."

"Suppose whoever took Noel's call in Tangier — Mr. X — decided to collect a million dollars worth of narcotics. A risky business, but not too risky. Suppose Mr. X jumped into his car, drove all night, then telephoned Noel from somewhere in the neighborhood."

"The times apparently match."

"Now I've got to make one or two suppositions. I put myself in Mr. X's place. Would I drive all the way to Erfoud before calling? I'd be anxious and nervous. I'd wonder whether Noel were still at the hotel, whether I were making the drive for nothing. I'd call from Ksar-es-Souk — to learn Noel's plans, to make whatever arrangements with Noel I had worked up during the night."

"That's reasonable enough."

"What would Mr. X do when he learned that Noel had left the hotel? The suppositions take on a sinister color. If Mr. X were determined to take the heroin, he'd start down the road from Ksar-es-Souk and pick a spot to wait for Noel."

"I see. Granting all this, what do you propose to do?"

"We go to Ksar-es-Souk, inquire at likely spots if anyone made a phone call to Erfoud at seven-thirty or eight in —" He stopped short. Ellen stood stiffly, her eyes fixed on something across the palm grove. He followed the direction of her gaze. "What are you looking at?"

She pointed. "See between those two tall clumps? That's the main road. A dark car just went by, a small dark car."

Darrell watched the gap through the palms for a few moments. A Moroccan rode by on a bicycle, djellaba flapping behind. "All the cars out here are small and dark," said Darrell.

Ellen turned him a sarcastic glance, but restrained whatever response had occurred to her.

Darrell asked politely, "Are you ready for breakfast?"

"Yes."

The austere elderly couple were already in the dining room, with toast and orange juice in front of them, an elaborate silver coffee urn on a service cart beside their table.

A waiter in a starched white jacket seated Ellen with a click of the heels, presented menus.

Darrell said, "You can have bacon and eggs, ham and eggs, omelettes of all kinds, herring, cheese, mixed grill —"

"Just tea, please."

"Tea? You'll starve."

Ellen shrugged, looked off out the window. Darrell hesitated, then ordered orange juice, toast, bacon and eggs for them both, with tea for Ellen, coffee for himself.

Jugs of orange juice in basins of crushed ice were set before them, a coffee urn and a china teapot wheeled up on a service cart. Covered dishes were carried in, served, the covers whisked off.

Ellen poured herself a cup of tea, sat sipping, looking out the window.

Darrell helped himself to toast, began to eat. Presently he asked, "Who's the moral coward now?"

Ellen said in a measured voice, "I'm not hungry."

Darrell nodded in profound understanding. "In that case, I apologize. You're not a moral coward."

Ellen wrenched her gaze away from the window. "Darn it," she muttered. "I am hungry. And now I've got to eat."

Darrell consoled her. "You won't feel quite so edgy."

Ellen savagely attacked the bacon and eggs. Ten minutes later she looked up from her empty plate. "There. You talked me into eating. A rather petty triumph. Are you pleased with it?"

"I'm glad you had your breakfast." He finished his coffee. Ellen again was looking stonily out the window. Darrell sighed. "I suppose we'd better think about leaving."

"Whenever you wish."

Half an hour later they drove away from the hotel — out to the main road, north beside the palm grove, up through a group of red sandstone pinnacles, out across the flint-covered desert.

Darrell said, "There can't be too many places in Ksar-es-Souk from which a person could telephone at seven-thirty in the morning. The obvious place would be the service station where we filled up last night. Mr. X's car would need gas too."

Ellen nodded distantly.

"We'll fill up again in Ksar-es-Souk, and ask questions at the same time."

Ksar-es-Souk appeared in the distance, a line of low tomato-red blocks against the dun background of the Atlas. At the outskirts of town, near the fork in the road, was the service station.

Darrell slowed the car. "Here's where we test my theories. Mr. X comes driving down from the mountains. It's seven-thirty in the morning; he's later than he wants to be, and he's anxious — perhaps Noel has already left Erfoud. He's also low on gas and here's a service station." He pulled into the station, stopped beside the pumps. From the office the attendant emerged, limping on a crippled leg; a short heavy-shouldered man, with black hair combed in a mid-Victorian swirl down over his forehead. He had careful inquisitive eyes in a bland face. *"Oui, monsieur?"*

"The language barrier again," said Darrell in disgust. He turned to Ellen. "You'll have to translate. Better have him fill the tank."

Ellen gave the necessary instructions; the attendant hobbled to the pumps. Ellen jumped out of the car, Darrell followed. She addressed a question to the attendant. Darrell watched his expression. He raised his eyebrows, looked rather queerly at Ellen, at Darrell, shrugged, shook his head, replied. Darrell could not decide whether his answer were positive or negative.

Ellen translated. "He says a clever man remembers only to count his change after his patrons leave; and so avoids getting into trouble."

Darrell took a five-thousand franc note from his wallet. "This may stimulate his memory."

The attendant took the note, pursing his lips reverently, appeared to concentrate. He spoke at length.

Ellen said grudgingly, "Your theories seem to be correct. A car stopped here early in the morning a month ago; the driver made a telephone call. This man was busy under the lubrication rack; his assistant took care of the car. He paid no particular attention and only remembers because of the telephone call to Erfoud, which as you supposed is not a usual occurrence."

"Well, we're on the right track," said Darrell. "Where is the assistant?"

Ellen inquired; the attendant, screwing the cap back on the gas tank, made a vague gesture, replied.

"He's not here," Ellen told Darrell. "He quit two weeks ago, and apparently went to Rabat."

"Confound it! Can this man describe the driver?"

Ellen asked, listened to the response. "He says he paid very little attention. He thinks there were two in the car, a man and a woman."

"A man *and* a woman?"

"That's what he says."

"Young or old?"

Ellen asked, received the response. "He doesn't know. He paid no attention."

"How about the car?"

There was the sequence of question and reply. Ellen hesitated, looked doubtfully at Darrell.

"Well?"

"He says it was a car like this one. He says he thought it was the same car when we drove up. He thought we were the same people."

"Well, obviously we're not. Damn! So near and yet so far. Isn't there anything else he remembers?"

Ellen inquired. The answer came; she translated. "He says he thinks the car drove off toward Erfoud."

"And that's all he knows?"

"Apparently."

"Does he know where we can locate the mechanic who quit?"

"I already asked him. He says no, the man was on his way back to France."

Darrell paid for the gas. "What a let-down. If only he had noticed *something*! Was the man big? Little? Fat? Thin?"

Ellen asked; the attendant shrugged, spoke.

"He says the man seemed about average size. He never saw his face, in fact paid no attention to him or the car."

Darrell started the car. "Well, that's that." He left the station, drove slowly back down the road toward Erfoud. "While I think of it, Duff drives this car, doesn't he?"

"Not often. I discourage it."

"Did he borrow it a month ago?"

"I don't think so. Are we going back to Erfoud?"

"No more than half-way, because the X's and Noel would have met before then."

"And what happened when they met — since you're theorizing?"

"Let's pretend we're the X's. We've been driving all night. We're planning to hijack a load of heroin. We're nervous. We want the money, but we don't want to be caught."

"We wouldn't stay here, on the flat area," said Ellen. "We'd go down the road farther — where we could see traffic coming from both directions."

"Right. We drive till we find a good spot. Noel may or may not expect us... No, he wouldn't know we're here. He thinks Mr. X gave the message to Arthur. He'll be looking in his rear-view mirror, watching for the FLN."

They returned back over the barren area. "Every minute, every kilometer we're more tense," said Darrell, "because we're not sure where we'll meet Noel. If he sees us, the game blows up; he's no fool; he knows we have no business here."

Ellen said woodenly, "If that's how we feel, then we've already decided to kill Noel. Because we can't have tales carried back to Tangier."

Darrell nodded. "That's undoubtedly what we've decided. Ambush."

The road dipped briefly into the valley, rose back to the desert, crossed a mile of barrens, then dropped again, winding in hairpin switch-backs through red sandstone bluffs down to the fertile green ribbon. Darrell jammed on the brakes. "Look. From here you can see the road behind, before it takes that dip. There's a car turning down now. Ahead you can see the road, not quite as well, but far enough for two or three minutes warning. Look, way down there — a bus. See it?"

"Yes."

Darrell parked at the side of the road, alighted. The sun, already intense, beat into his face. To the right was the valley; to the left a ledge of rusty sandstone, a wind-tormented crag, a wide area of flint-covered desert. Ahead the road curved sharply down to the valley floor. Ellen came to stand beside him. They heard the bus approach, wheezing and grinding up the slope.

"Here comes the truck," said Darrell. "We're waiting for it. We're ready. It's coming slowly, pulling up the hill in low."

The bus nosed around the turn; a row of curious dark faces looked down at them; then the bus was past, roaring off toward Ksar-es-Souk.

"So," said Darrell. "I stopped the truck. I jumped on the running-board, or maybe I stood here and shot. Noel's foot would slide off the accelerator. One way or another we've got the truck. We've got to work fast. I throw out the heroin. You pile it in the car — in the rear compartment, behind the seat, on the floor, anywhere. We're in a frenzy. There's traffic along here, we can't loiter. We're exultant too. A million dollars! But now, here's the truck, and a body. How to hide the horrid deed? We don't want to be discovered. So —" he looked off to the left "— we drive it off the road, out across the rocks." He walked out, scanning the landscape. Ellen followed.

"We could drive it out here, if we didn't care about tires — and of course we don't. We'd head out behind that big jut of rock. Nobody would have a reason to come out here. A truck could rest fifty years…"

They climbed over the ledge of sandstone, walked behind the crag. The sun glared on their heads; rocks rolled and twisted underfoot. Nothing grew except little green balls of lichen, dry and spongy.

"No truck," said Ellen. "The theory isn't working so well."

Darrell looked around the barren waste. "No. Apparently not. Unless —" he pointed. "There's a gully over here."

They walked across the desert. The gully opened abruptly before them, a harsh steep-sided watercourse, now dry, draining into the river valley. Below them a gray dump-truck lay on its side, battered and crumpled.

"You wait up here," said Darrell.

Ellen waited. Darrell clambered down to the truck, looked into the cab, jerked his head back. He walked around the truck, then struggled back up the slope. Ellen waited silently.

"Noel's in there. What's left of him." They stood looking down at the truck, the heat of the sunshine tingling against their skin. The truck lay asprawl and clumsy like a dead dinosaur. And in the cab, the withered brain of the dead beast, Noel.

"Well, we've found him," said Darrell.

"I'm sorry," said Ellen. She hesitated, then reached over and took his hand. "I'm really sorry."

"It's no surprise, no great shock. I'm sorry too — but it was the chance he took."

Ellen stiffened. "Listen." Darrell had also heard the faint sound of rock touching rock. He looked around. From the direction of the road came three men. One wore a rough brown djellaba. The second wore baggy trousers and a green pull-over: Slip-Slip. The third, in smart gray gabardine and a red fez, was Abd Allah el Kazim.

CHAPTER XIII

THE MOROCCANS CAME to look over the edge of the gully. Abd Allah el Kazim gestured; Slip-Slip scrambled down to the truck. El Kazim turned to Darrell. "We meet again."

Darrell agreed guardedly. He glanced toward the road; the crag and the low sandstone ridge hid it from view. "So you knew the truck was here all the time."

El Kazim shook his head, teeth glistening. "No. We did not know. But we knew that you would lead us to it. Ever since you first arrived in Tangier, we have watched you. Because we knew that you would bring us here."

"I didn't bring you to much," said Darrell. "Just Noel."

"Where is the heroin?" El Kazim asked the question casually, as if he were inquiring the time of day.

"I suppose that whoever killed Noel took it. I don't know, I really don't care."

El Kazim turned him a quick glance, lips drawn back in his feral grin. "You don't care to know who killed your brother?"

"Noel played with fire. He got burned. He knew it was hot."

"But he was your brother, the son of your father, your own blood!" His glance went to Ellen, returned to Darrell.

"I'm sick of the whole business," said Darrell. "I've found Noel. He's beyond any help I'm able to give him."

El Kazim laughed politely. "A good Moslem could never rest until he had dealt with the man who did such a foul deed." His glance once again rested on Ellen.

"That may be," said Darrell shortly. "Let's go, Ellen."

El Kazim held up his hand. "Just one moment, before you go. I am curious."

"About what?"

"How did you know the truck was here? Did Miss McKinstry tell you?"

"No, of course not."

"Then how did you know? In all the great desert, you found this place."

"It seemed reasonable that someone had stopped Noel along this road. I picked the first likely spot."

El Kazim nodded, eyes traveling back and forth between Darrell and Ellen. "You are clever. But, you see, we are as clever as you. Never forget that."

Slip-Slip clambered back up out of the gully. He reported in guttural Arabic, spat disgustedly into the dirt. El Kazim replied softly, almost jocularly. All three turned to look at Darrell and Ellen.

"We're going," said Darrell.

"A moment, please do not go yet. One or two things I wish to ask you."

"Well?" Darrell waited half-turned away, with Ellen pressed against his back.

"Who did Noel call from Erfoud?"

"I don't know."

"But you lie, American," said el Kazim, grinning. "You lie."

"I'm telling you the truth."

"But you stopped at the service station in Ksar-es-Souk. We watched you, and we stopped too. You paid five thousand francs, we paid five thousand francs. A month ago a man and a woman came from Tangier in a black sports car. In Miss McKinstry's car. If you are not lying, then you are stupid."

"I don't understand you," said Darrell coldly. Ellen's body felt tense and tight; her breath came fast.

El Kazim nodded toward Ellen. "She understands well enough. Noel telephoned her. He made two telephone calls from Erfoud. Is it not clear? He called the Balmoral Hotel. Aktouf assured us that he took no message. We have suspected Miss McKinstry for some time. She took the message, she came in her car, with someone else. They killed Noel, took the heroin."

Darrell laughed. "It sounds well, but it just doesn't make sense. In the first place Noel made three calls, not two."

"No, Mr. Hutson. We also have consulted the clerk. He tells us Noel made only two calls."

"You ask him now, and he'll tell you differently."

El Kazim shook his head. "Let us be sensible. There is no need for further waste of time. I will ask Miss McKinstry, pleasantly and politely, where she has taken the heroin. I am sure she will tell me, because she remembers the difficulties poor Mr. Aktouf discovered... I will ask. Where is the heroin, Miss McKinstry? Don't answer hastily. Think well. There is ample time, and we are quite alone; no one will overhear."

Ellen said nothing.

"Where is the heroin, Miss McKinstry?"

"I haven't any idea," said Ellen.

"Who came with you to Ksar-es-Souk a month ago?"

"No one. Because I didn't come."

"Please think hard, Miss McKinstry." El Kazim turned, looked here and there over the desert. He spoke in Arabic; Slip-Slip trotted away. The other reached into his pouch, brought forth an automatic pistol, ostentatiously snapped a shell into the firing chamber.

"Are you thinking, Miss McKinstry? Think quickly. My friend is getting certain helps for us from the car."

"I don't know anything," said Ellen. "If you hope to frighten me with that ridiculous gun, you're mistaken." She turned, walked toward the road.

"Stop!" called el Kazim hoarsely. "Stop. Or you will be shot."

Ellen made no answer, continued.

El Kazim muttered over his shoulder; his aide raised the gun, aiming high on Ellen's thigh. "Ellen!" cried Darrell.

Ellen looked over her shoulder. She saw the leveled gun, threw herself to the ground. At the same instant the Moroccan fired.

Something peculiar happened to Darrell. The world became a different world, and he was a new creature. He threw himself at the

Moroccan. His goal was the throat; his hands hooked to claw through flesh. At contact with the burly body, other reflexes came into play. The Moroccan flailed with the gun; Darrell struck a terrible blow with his right fist, half-jumping off the ground with the thrust of his leg. The Moroccan's head rolled askew, he tottered backwards. The gun dropped. Darrell lurched for it, looked behind, recovered himself. Abd Allah el Kazim came dancing forward like a crow, pulling out his own gun. Darrell rushed with head down, almost on all fours, running to keep from falling on his face. He struck el Kazim with a charging football block; el Kazim toppled back over the edge of the gully, rolled, tumbled, thrashed to the bottom. Darrell turned to the Moroccan, now crawling on hands and knees to the gun. Darrell ran forward, kicked him under the jaw, bent for the gun.

He heard Ellen's scream. A shadow loomed over him: Slip-Slip. Darrell glimpsed steel; he dropped to the ground, rolled. Slip-Slip spit and hissed, dancing over the rocks with a fluttering of the djellaba, leaning forward with his knife. Darrell rolled away, jumped to his feet, picking up lumps of rock in each hand. He threw with all his power; the rock, grape-fruit size, struck Slip-Slip in the chest. From a different angle came another rock, which missed, but which distracted Slip-Slip's attention. Ellen had returned. Darrell threw his second rock; Slip-Slip dodged, backed away.

Darrell picked up the gun; Slip-Slip took to his heels. The older Moroccan lay on his face, hands clenching and unclenching. Ellen stood uncertainly a few yards away, carrying stones in her hands. She smiled at Darrell — a ghostly smile of encouragement. Darrell made a meaningless gesture, went to look over the side of the gully. El Kazim, eyes wild and red as pomegranate kernels, was half-way up the slope, crawling with gun in hand, dragging one leg, blood streaming down his cheek. At the sight of Darrell he squealed, raised his arm, fired. Darrell jumped back; the shot whistled past his ear.

Darrell pushed a round black rock twice the size of his head over the edge of the gully. There was a rumble, a clatter, dying away in a diminishing rattle of small stones. Darrell glanced cautiously over the edge. El Kazim lay crumpled at the bottom of the gully. Unconscious or shamming? Darrell could not be certain.

"Best to shoot him," said Ellen huskily.

"I can't."

"When I think of what he wanted to do —"

"Let's go," said Darrell, but Ellen pulled at his arm.

"Look at his head!"

El Kazim's head hung far back, twisted so that he looked along his shoulder.

"If he's not dead he's awfully sick," said Darrell. There was motion to the side; the older Moroccan was tensed against the ground, staring at them.

Darrell took Ellen's arm. "Let's go."

They walked back across the rock-strewn desert. Around the side of the crag Slip-Slip watched them. The older man rose to his feet, hobbled to the edge of the gully, looked down. He beckoned; Slip-Slip went to him.

Darrell and Ellen returned to the road. Beside the Mercedes-Benz were el Kazim's Citroën and a small black Fiat.

Ellen looked sidewise at Darrell. "You were right," said Darrell. "You saw a small black car this morning."

"I thought I saw one," said Ellen. "It may not have been this one, of course."

"This one is close enough. Another thing — last night I made up my mind to ask you something, at the right time. Maybe this is the right time, maybe it isn't. But I'll ask anyway. Will you marry me?"

"It's the right time," said Ellen. "Almost any time would have been right."

"Then you will?"

"Of course. Why else would I try so hard to hate you?"

"That's illogical," said Darrell, "but I think I know what you mean." He lifted the Moroccan's automatic — a new Mauser — snapped the safety, put it in his pocket. "I'll keep this for a souvenir. It might come in handy, who knows?" They climbed into the car. Darrell started the engine, shifted, they were away.

Ellen kissed his cheek. "Thank you for protecting me."

Darrell grinned. "Thanks for drawing the fire."

"I was hysterical."

"But we're both alive, and with all our arms and legs, thank heaven!"

"Now what do we do?"

"Police, I suppose."

She sighed. "There'll be no end of trouble."

"Probably, but I can't leave Noel's body out there in the desert."

The road dwindled behind them; they passed Ksar-es-Souk, started up the approach to the Atlas.

"Darrell," Ellen said thoughtfully.

"Yes?"

"El Kazim thought I had killed Noel."

"So he said."

"It sounds reasonable, doesn't it?"

"In a way."

"Do you think I did?"

"I've considered the possibility."

"What if I had?"

"It would set me quite a problem. I don't think you did."

"Why not?"

"First, the three telephone calls. Second, you went to the service station with me, quite openly. If you were Mrs. X — I should say Miss X — you'd be afraid of recognition. So far as I could see, it never occurred to you."

"Well, it wasn't I, so you don't have the problem. And if it had been I, I'd tell you. Then I'd weep, and say I was sorry, that I only did it to spite Arthur, and you'd forgive me."

"Yes, I probably would."

They rolled back over the Atlas: past Rich, up over the Pass of the She-Camel to Midelt, down through the Col du Zad to Azrou, and the sun hung low over the great plain of the Maghreb.

In Meknes they ate dinner, refueled, turned the Mercedes-Benz north, and at midnight coasted down out of the hills into the bright crescent of Tangier. Ellen pressed close to Darrell.

"What's the trouble?"

"Coming back to Tangier. I feel tight inside, and hard and angry… Darrell, must I go home?"

"Of course not. You're coming with me. Now and always."

She sighed. "I don't want to go back to that house. For eight years I've planned to kill Arthur, and I can't get it out of my mind."

"Sh," said Darrell. "In a few days we'll be leaving, and it'll all be behind you."

They turned up Calle Miranda, parked. At the Miranda Hotel Darrell booked a room for Ellen, ignoring the bland manner of the clerk.

At her door she kissed him. "Give me time for a shower."

"Fifteen minutes?"

"Ten is enough. But I may still be wet."

CHAPTER XIV

THE NEXT MORNING DARRELL went to the headquarters of the Sûreté Nationale, on the second floor of an airy white building at the bottom of Boulevard Pasteur. In the outer office a dozen men and women waited, while behind the counter an unhurried functionary examined, marked, stamped, approved, disapproved or rejected the forms they had filled out — applications for travel permits, exit visas, any of the other special documents required by citizens and aliens alike.

Darrell went to the far end of the room, signaled to a fat young man in sun-tans, who without troubling to rise from his chair pointed to the clerk. Reluctant to explain his business in front of a dozen bystanders, Darrell made a more peremptory gesture. The fat young man paused, glumly heaved himself from his chair, approached. "What do you want, sir?"

"I want to report a homicide. A death."

The fat young man looked at Darrell with increased interest. "You kill somebody?"

"No. I want to speak to the officer in charge of such matters."

"Please, one minute." He disappeared into a back room. A moment passed. He emerged, lumbered forward to open the gate in the counter. "Captain Goulidja," he hissed under his breath, "you will speak to him."

Behind a green metal desk sat a short thick man of Napoleonic mien. Ringlets of mingled black and gray clustered over his broad forehead. He wore an expression of mildly amused skepticism, as if to warn malefactors, actual or putative, that their guile had been foreseen and discounted. He held out his hand.

"Your passport, please."

Darrell handed over the green booklet. Captain Goulidja flicked it open with an expert hand, assimilated what information it contained with an air of faint astonishment, placed it carefully down on his desk. "What did you wish, please? You report a death?"

"My brother Noel has been missing for a month. I came to Tangier to find out what was wrong. I learned that he had been carrying guns to the Algerian rebels —"

"The FLN," interjected Captain Goulidja, without emphasis.

"He wrote me a letter from Erfoud."

"Ah yes, Erfoud."

"I went to Erfoud, I made some inquiries, which convinced me he had run into trouble. Yesterday I checked the road from Erfoud to Ksar-es-Souk, finally found my brother. He was dead, in a truck which had been driven into a ravine. I left him there, and last night returned to Tangier. If you will give me a map, I will show you where he is to be found."

Captain Goulidja nodded perfunctorily, leaned back in his chair. "I see. And your position is what?"

"My position?" asked Darrell in surprise. "I have no position. I came here to report the death of my brother."

Captain Goulidja shook his head in polite condolence. "He is an American citizen also?"

"Yes."

"And so you wish us to investigate this death?"

Darrell inspected the placid face in perplexity. Was the captain practicing a local variety of one-upmanship, or merely, in all innocence, seeking information? A third possibility occurred to him: Captain Goulidja might be collecting his thoughts. Darrell said in a formal voice, "The investigation is your concern. I suppose you have your regulations."

"Yes. We have regulations, just as in the United States. And why have you come to us? You wish us to find the killer of your brother?"

Darrell moved in his chair. "Does it make any difference what I want? My brother is dead — killed, murdered. I am reporting this death to you because I assume the law of Morocco requires me to do so."

"Yes," said Captain Goulidja. "That is right. Why did you not report to Erfoud?"

"Because I am staying here in Tangier, at the Miranda Hotel."

Captain Goulidja made a note. "You are carrying guns to Algeria too?" he asked casually.

"No. I arrived here recently. The date is in my passport. I came because my brother wrote me he was in trouble. This is the letter."

Captain Goulidja read the letter with amused incredulity — or so it seemed. He put the letter beside the passport, leaned back in his chair, looked up at the ceiling. "I will say that we have heard something of this case. We know many things, but in these times we must walk with care. There is much trouble in the world, is there not?"

"A great deal of trouble, I would say."

Captain Goulidja nodded. "What is right, what is wrong…" he held out his hands, raised his eyebrows, smiled. "It is for men wiser than I to say."

Darrell realized that Captain Goulidja was imparting information with great delicacy, talking around the circumference of his meaning, defining his theme without ever touching it.

"It is very sad for you," Captain Goulidja continued. "Such things happen, of course. As you know there is great international concern over Algeria. There are negotiations. The French are being asked to take their garrisons from Morocco. There is always much talk of arms traffic; it is a shame. The French stop ships, they force down airplanes. It is not legal, but what can we do?" He shook his head dolefully. "There is much trouble in North Africa now. We know many things. But we must be careful."

Darrell nodded briefly. "About Noel —"

"I will make the investigation. But perhaps it will be quiet. A non-political matter." He pounded the table lightly with his fist. "In Morocco, there is law, just as in the United States. So we forget nothing, we make the full investigation. You are not leaving Tangier?"

"No. Not for a few days. I want to get my brother's body." Darrell stopped, an image of Noel, as he had been in his youth, coming before his eyes: feckless, lazy, good-humored, boundless in his fine conceits. This flamboyant, slightly ridiculous Noel was truly dead. "I want to ship him home."

Captain Goulidja stared out the window, out over the bright blue harbor. He turned back brusquely. "Very good. Wait one moment please." He took up his telephone, called a number, waited, spoke in Arabic. The conversation continued several minutes. At one point he turned to Darrell. "Where exactly is the truck?"

Darrell explained with as much precision as possible; Captain Goulidja returned to the telephone, the conversation continued. Finally he hung up, reached in his desk, brought out a pad of paper, took a fountain pen from his pocket. "Now. I must ask questions."

Two hours later Darrell returned to the hotel. As he arrived Ellen drove up in the Mercedes-Benz, three suitcases on the seat beside her. "I'm moved out," she said flatly. She seemed to be avoiding Darrell's eyes.

"What's the trouble?" he asked.

She got out of the car, wearing a dark green frock, with a white collar close around her neck. "I've just had an upsetting quarrel."

Darrell lifted her suitcases to the sidewalk. "With Arthur?"

"No. Just Duff. He called me all kinds of names."

"Because of me?"

"Yes, partly. He doesn't like you."

"It doesn't matter. How long does it take to get married?"

"Two days, I think."

"We'll start the process this afternoon. And we'll go to the consulate also, in case there's any red tape."

She shook her head. "It won't work, Darrell. I can't do it. You go home. I'm going to London and get a job."

"Good heavens. What brought this on?"

She looked sullenly up the street. "Good sense. I'm not in love with you, you're not in love with me."

"I see," said Darrell.

"It's been propinquity. The moon, the palm trees. Emotions, guns going off, more propinquity…"

Darrell considered a moment. "If we get married there'll be nothing but propinquity."

"I know."

"Do you object?"

"No." She spoke in a muffled voice. "But I can't come back with you, a bedraggled waif you picked up in Tangier."

"I won't go back without you."

"You won't?"

"Not unless you make it clear that you don't want to come."

She laughed. "That's asking a lot. I don't think I can do it."

Darrell heaved a deep sigh. "That's that, then. Has Duff been putting those ideas in your head?"

"Not altogether. They've been there."

"Are they gone now?"

"Yes, I suppose so."

"Good. I'll take these suitcases in, then we'll go for lunch. Some place cheerful."

Fifteen minutes later they were high on the top floor of the Hotel Velasquez, sitting by a window, with the wide blue, white and yellow panorama below. She reached across the table, squeezed his hand. "You're very calm and settling, Darrell. I feel much better."

"I don't feel calm. I'd like to punch Duff's nose."

"If you persist in marrying me, he'll be your brother-in-law."

"I'll have to take the bad with the good. After all, you don't know what you're getting into either."

"I'll take my chances. I'll be polite and ladylike and no one will suspect what a monster I really am...Tell me about the police."

"There's not much to tell. They're bringing in the body. I telephoned my father; he wants me to ship it home. I'll have to make arrangements."

Ellen twisted the stem of the wine-glass between her fingers. "Did they ask you many questions?"

"About what you'd expect."

She looked into her glass, at the satin disk of wine. "What did you tell them?"

"Everything I knew. Except about Noel's cargo being heroin. They'll have to find that out from someone else."

Ellen seemed on the point of speaking; she moved uncomfortably in her seat.

"What's the trouble?" Darrell asked.

"I'm wondering — suppose the police think I did it, or helped do it?"

"It's a possibility."

"That I did it?"

"That the police will suspect you."

Ellen laughed shakily. "Well, I didn't. I haven't even killed Arthur, whom I quite desperately want to kill." She sighed. "Darrell, you've changed my life. Since I can't convince you to be evil, I'll have to give up my wickedness and become a nice American housewife — or at least pretend to be — and spank our children for naughtiness I secretly approve of."

Darrell looked at his watch. "Before we can have children we've got to be married. Let's go get the license, or whatever it's called here."

"What time is it?"

"Two o'clock."

Ellen nodded. "Good. We've got time. I've got to go back to the house this afternoon. There's an auctioneer coming out to look at the furniture."

"Would you like me to come?"

She shook her head. "It's a dismal business. I'd much rather do it by myself."

"Whatever you'd like to keep, we'll ship home."

"Home?" She looked surprised for a moment. "Yes, I've got a home now, haven't I?" She reflected. "It would be nice to keep the grandfather clock. And the piano. And the books."

"Doesn't Duff have anything to say?"

She laughed shortly. "Duff owes me twenty thousand pounds. He has nothing to say."

They drove to the rambling old municipal building, roamed tall dark corridors, checked dozens of doors with triplicate inscriptions in French, Spanish and Arabic. They found the appropriate office, filled out appropriate forms, displayed documents, paid the fee and received the marriage license, likewise printed in three languages.

They returned to where they had parked the car. "I've got to see that damned auctioneer," said Ellen. "What are you going to do?"

"One thing and another. Perhaps I'll go down to the Hotel de los Dos Continentes and pick up Noel's belongings. A melancholy task, but it's got to be done. I'll meet you when you're finished with the auctioneer."

"Very well. Where?"

"The Masquerade?"

Ellen wrinkled her nose. "All right. The Masquerade. At six o'clock. Can I drop you down to Noel's hotel?"

"I'll take a cab."

Ellen said, "Let me see the marriage license once more. Just to be sure it's real."

"It's real. And I'm real."

"I know you're real." She kissed him. "I'm very lucky, Darrell. I promise you I'll try to be good, whether my heart's in it or not." She laughed. "I've never been so excited!"

"Until six," said Darrell grinning. "And don't get into any trouble."

He watched her walk to the car, slim and jaunty, her blonde-brown cap shining in the Tangier sunlight. She waved at him, then she was gone.

Darrell walked to the Boulevard Pasteur. He visited several shops, made a purchase in the last. The time was now almost five o'clock. The Hotel de los Dos Continentes and Noel's clothes could wait until tomorrow. He walked up to the Hotel Miranda. He showered, changed into his dark suit; at quarter to six he crossed the street to the Masquerade Bar.

Phil Beresford greeted him with a careless wave of the hand. Darrell slipped up on a bar stool; Phil shook his head. "That's Mr. Burdette's throne. He's out in the kitchen selling Mama a Rolls-Royce. Move over one."

Darrell ordered a highball; Phil flipped ice into a glass. "What's new? That brother of yours showed his guilty face yet?"

"His face wasn't guilty when I saw it."

Phil stopped dramatically with whiskey bottle in mid-air. "You found him?"

Darrell nodded. "Dead."

Phil mixed the highball with reverence. "Well, that's too bad. No particular surprise of course. Where did you locate him?"

"In a truck a hundred yards off the road, down toward the desert."

"Hijack, eh?" He set out the highball.

"I wouldn't know for sure."

"You tell the police?"

"This morning."

"Who did you talk to?"

"Captain Goulidja."

"I know him. Not a bad fellow. But he won't move on anything stronger than a wife-beating until he gets official policy. Do you mind if I tell a journalist friend of mine? A scoop's a scoop."

"Go ahead."

"By 'journalist friend', naturally I mean T-Bone." He ducked under the bar, looked into the Balmoral lobby. "Hey, Lucky! Call T-Bone, tell her I want to talk to her. A hot news story."

He ducked back under the bar. Mr. Burdette emerged from the kitchen, wiping his mouth. "Here, Mr. Burdette! Fingers in the cookie jar again!"

"Please, Phil," said Mr. Burdette, "let me enjoy your last few days."

Phil shook his head. "It's bad enough you plundering the larder; don't make me get sentimental about it."

"Are you leaving?" Darrell asked Phil.

Phil nodded. "I got my notice. New owner to the building wants to run the bar himself."

"That's too bad."

"I don't mind. I been here too long. The wild geese is flying south. I'm leaving Mama with Mr. Burdette. They'll make out fine. Me and T-Bone will be far away, dancing to the music of castanets and flutes."

"Have you told Mama about this?" asked Mr. Burdette.

"Mama don't need to be told. She *knows* these things."

Mrs. Phil said in a neutral voice, just under Phil's elbow, "You're wanted on the phone."

"Who, me? Yes sir. I mean, yes, ma'am. I'm coming."

Phil presently returned, pounding his temples with his fists. "That T-Bone. Tact and grace of a cow in mud. Sending Mama to fetch me to the phone." He turned to Darrell. "She'll be right down. She just wanted to know what's so all-fired important."

"You told her?"

"I gave her the bare outlines."

"Was she surprised?"

"You're asking me to read T-Bone's mind? That's like asking a blind ape to read Egyptian hieroglyphics, with no Rosetta Stone."

"She doesn't write these things herself, does she?"

Phil shook his head. "T-Bone's the roving reporter. She passes on the tip, and if it's any good they slip her a few thousand francs. It went pretty high when she found a certain Swede actress staying incognito in the Balmoral. Here she comes. Brace yourself."

T-Bone slipped in from the Balmoral wearing a tight black jersey blouse and a soft pleated skirt the color of old whiskey — almost a match for her shoulder-length hair.

"Darrell! You've found Noel! And he's dead!"

"My word," squeaked Mr. Burdette. "Is this true?"

Darrell assented politely. "I'm afraid so."

"We're very sorry," said T-Bone. "It was the Algerians who did it?"

"I don't know," said Darrell. "The police are investigating now."

T-Bone made careful notes on a paper napkin, using a ball-point pen lent her fatalistically by Phil. "Careful, T-Bone, don't lick the point. You'll get streaks all up and down your tongue."

Darrell glanced at his watch. Six-thirty. Where was Ellen? Late. Why should she be late? Something heavy slid down into his stomach. Why should Ellen be late? A dozen possible reasons — one of which terrified him.

Darrell jumped to his feet. "Phil, if Ellen McKinstry comes in, tell her I'll be right back."

"Okay, will do."

Darrell ran out into the street, looked for a cab. He started down toward the Place de France, halted, ran into the Hotel Miranda. With maddening deliberation the clerk gave him his key. Darrell bounded up the steps to his room, pocketed the Mauser automatic he had brought back from Erfoud, ran downstairs. A cruising taxi came past; Darrell flagged it, gave the address of the McKinstry villa on Calle Costanza. "Fast," he said. "Hurry."

They raced up the hill, the little motor whirring like a power-saw.

Darrell pointed out the house. "Wait for me."

He jumped from the cab. The Mercedes-Benz was parked in the driveway. At the curb was Arthur Upshaw's big pale blue Chrysler, across the street a dusty black Citroën.

Darrell stood looking at the house. Smoke was rising from the chimney. The evening was rather warm.

Time seemed to move slowly. Darrell drifted to the house. It loomed larger and larger before him, filling the sky as he mounted the front steps. He tried the door, it was locked. He went along the porch to a window, looked in, but the curtains were drawn. He listened, and seemed to hear a murmur of voices.

He put out his finger to ring the bell, stopped short. He jumped down off the porch, raced around to the back, climbed wooden steps to the service porch. The door was also locked. By standing on the rail, reaching to the side he could grasp the sill of an open window. He made an awkward leap, wriggled through the window, landing face down on the floor. He picked himself up, took the gun from his pocket, snapped off the safety, opened the door into the kitchen. Here he stopped to listen.

The voices were clearer but still inaudible. Darrell started forward, then hesitated, uncomfortably aware of his position. If conditions were all in order, he would appear ridiculous. He put his hand and the gun into his coat-pocket, eased open the swinging door, slowly entered the polished walnut and silver-gleaming dining room.

There was silence — a heavy cotton-wool silence. Then a sharp gasp. Then came Arthur Upshaw's voice, quiet and controlled. "She's fainted."

Conditions were not all in order.

Duff said, "Look here, Arthur, I don't think —"

"Shut up. Get some cold water."

Duff came out of the study. He saw Darrell, stopped stock-still.

Darrell pointed the gun. "Back," he said in a guttural voice.

Duff backed into the study. Darrell followed. Arthur Upshaw looked up, stern and scowling. Jilali sat on the sofa, smoking a cigarette. The fire burnt cheerfully. Ellen sat in a kitchen chair, wrists lashed behind the back with cellophane tape. Heavy cord bound her waist, thighs and ankles to the chair. Her legs were bare, the skirt pulled high up over her knees. Arthur Upshaw held a poker, white-gray with heat, smoking gently. One of Ellen's knees showed a long red mark.

Darrell stood in the doorway, pointing the gun, unable to speak. No one moved. Smoke curled up from Jilali's cigarette. Ten seconds passed, twenty seconds. Arthur Upshaw gently straightened his back, stood erect, the poker hanging loosely in his grip.

Darrell finally spoke. "Listen carefully. I'll kill you if you don't do exactly what I say. There won't be a second chance. Do you understand? Answer me. Do you understand?"

Duff nodded dumbly.

"Answer me," said Darrell.

"I understand," said Duff.

"I understand," said Jilali equably.

Darrell looked at Arthur Upshaw.

Arthur Upshaw nodded, his mouth compressed into a length of white string.

Darrell said slowly, "Turn around, Upshaw."

Upshaw swung the poker a fraction of an inch. The gun pointed at his middle. He turned to face the fire. The firelight glowed, cast ruddy shadows on his face.

"Drop the poker."

The poker clattered on the bricks. He said contemptuously, "You're making a bloody damn fool of yourself."

"Duff, go to the wall, at the other side of the fireplace. Put your hands on the wall."

Duff obeyed.

"Jilali, put your hands in the air. Stand up. Turn around. Walk into the corner. Lean against the wall."

Jilali, cigarette in hand, went to the corner with an air of boredom.

"Upshaw — put your hands out and lean on the wall."

Arthur Upshaw obeyed without comment.

Darrell surveyed the three. "If any of you makes the slightest move — so much as turns a head, I'll shoot to kill. I'm aching for the excuse."

He listened at the door, concerned that there might be others in the house. The house was still.

Ellen was conscious; she smiled at him, a ghastly thin grin. Darrell asked her, "Are there any more?"

"No. Just those three."

Darrell went slowly to the desk, opened a drawer, never taking his eyes from the three men. A glance showed him a pair of scissors. He took it, walked slowly to Ellen, cautiously cut the tape. She brought her hands in front of her, rubbed her wrists.

Darrell gave her the scissors. "Cut yourself loose."

Feebly, hands trembling, she did so, rose swaying to her feet.

Darrell decided that Jilali was the one most likely to be carrying a gun. He said, "Jilali, hold your hands in the air. Walk backward, toward me…Don't move, Upshaw. Don't even quiver…Stop, Jilali. Sit down in the chair, put your arms behind you. Ellen, get that tape. Tie his wrists…Good. Now search him for a gun."

Ellen removed a small automatic from his coat-pocket. Darrell took it, examined it, snapped a shell into the firing chamber. "Can you use this?"

"Of course," said Ellen in a husky voice.

"It's cocked, ready to go off if you pull the trigger."

"I know."

"Keep it pointed at Upshaw…Duff, lie face down on the floor."

Darrell warily taped Duff's wrists, his ankles. "Now, Upshaw, face down on the floor."

"She killed your brother, you ruddy fool," said Upshaw savagely. "She's playing you for a goat!"

"Down on your face."

"What do you think you're up to with this monkey-business?"

Darrell came cautiously forward; Upshaw grudgingly lowered himself to the floor. He was taped, wrist and ankle.

Darrell stood looking at them. Ellen came to stand beside him.

"How many times did they burn you?"

"Just once…What are you going to do?"

"I don't know. At first I planned to kill them."

Darrell picked up the poker, put it into the fire. The three men watched him with fascinated eyes. Duff raised his head, called out in a hoarse voice: "Help!"

Darrell balled a handkerchief, thrust it into Duff's mouth. Duff spat it out, tried to bite, thrashed on the floor. Darrell rapped him with the muzzle of the gun, tied the handkerchief in a haphazard gag.

The poker was hot. "You three are lucky that I came when I did. You only had time to burn her once…Perhaps I ought to do what you might have done…"

Ellen clutched his arm. "Don't touch them, Darrell. Don't burn them."

"No? Why not?"

"I don't know. I can't explain. They're too horrible to touch."

Darrell grinned. "A little reminder?"

"No. Please don't. It's not because I'm merciful. It's just that — I can't explain. I want to get out of here. I don't want to breathe the same air they breathe."

"Just as you say. Do you have everything you want?"

"Yes. Please, let's go."

Darrell inspected the three men. Duff glared, Upshaw watched coldly, Jilali looked at him with mild reproach, a hint of derision.

"Ellen knows nothing of your heroin, nor do I. Please leave us out of your future plans."

Upshaw opened his mouth, closed it with a snap.

"My information is different," said Jilali.

"Your information is that a man and a woman in a black sports car came into Ksar-es-Souk the morning Noel was killed. That's all the information you have."

"It's enough to work on," said Jilali.

"You work somewhere else from now on." He turned away, took Ellen's hand. "Does your knee hurt?"

"A little. Not badly."

Darrell put the gun in his pocket. He took a last look at the three men, then turned. They left the house. The taxi-driver looked up sleepily. Darrell paid him off.

He drove the Mercedes-Benz back down the hill. "Where do you want to go?"

"I don't care. I was so glad to see you, Darrell, you'll never realize." She started to cry, then angrily wiped her face with her arm.

"I suppose they wanted their blasted heroin."

She nodded. "Jilali told Arthur that I'd killed Noel."

"What his men told him yesterday."

"I told them I didn't, they wouldn't believe me."

Darrell patted her. "I can't imagine Duff being a party to that kind of thing. The others yes. But Duff… After all, he's your brother."

"He does what Arthur tells him," said Ellen. "He can't help himself. And I suppose he thought I'd taken his heroin."

Darrell parked on the Place de France, in front of a drug store. "Let me see your knee." He examined the angry red blister. "I'll get some salve and some gauze. I think that's about all we can do for it."

He returned with salve, gauze, adhesive tape, and made a neat bandage. "Thank you," Ellen said weakly.

He patted her face. "Now, I've got something nice for you. Hold out your hand."

"What is it?"

"It's in this box."

She opened the box, took out the ring — a single square diamond on a platinum band. "Darrell, when I think how wicked I've been to you..."

"Let's go somewhere quiet and romantic. We'll drink a bottle of champagne, and then if you're hungry —"

"Oh no," said Ellen. "I feel as if I never could eat again. But I'd like to drink and drink... No, on second thought I think not. I'm too tired. In fact — I'm going to be sick."

Leaning out of the car, oblivious to the stares of passers-by, she vomited into the gutter.

"Darn," muttered Darrell. "I wasted my handkerchief on Duff."

"Never mind," she said faintly. "Drive away from here. I feel an awful fool."

"I'm the fool," said Darrell. "I should have taken you to the hotel and put you in bed."

"I don't want to go to bed... I feel better now. What a thing to do. I'm ashamed of myself."

"You've been under a terrible strain."

She nodded listlessly. "I know."

They went to a dimly lit restaurant at the crest of the hill. A girl in a red and yellow Berber costume served Ellen a Tom Collins, Darrell a highball.

"And still the problem remains," said Ellen. "Who's got the heroin, but I don't care any more. I'll be so happy to leave here."

"Tomorrow we'll go to the consulate. Undoubtedly there's a dozen documents to fill out."

Ellen examined her ring with a fond expression. "What a fool I've been. I really don't deserve you, Darrell. I won't badger you about ethics and morals any more. It's clearly better to be good than bad."

"You've summed it up very well," said Darrell. "I nearly killed three men tonight. I suppose that's bad…I don't know what stopped me. Squeamishness, I suppose."

"Let's not talk of it. It's all strange and blurred, as if it never happened. And I'm hungry enough now."

There was a dining room adjacent to the bar, hung with Berber rugs, scimitars, and long fantastic rifles. They sat on cushions of bright goatskin and were served Moroccan food: barbecued lamb, couscous with slivers of chicken in a bright yellow sauce.

Returning down the hill, Darrell slowed two blocks from Calle Miranda, coasted to a halt. "What's the trouble?" asked Ellen.

"This business has me worried. They're loose by now. Upshaw's upset, Duff is peevish, Jilali has lost face. Suppose they're waiting for us in front of the hotel? It's dark under those trees."

"I don't think they'd bother tonight. They're probably sick of the whole thing themselves."

"I'm not going to take any chances." He drove another block, parked. "I'll reconnoiter."

He went to the corner, looked around. The sign MASQUERADE was cut into sizzling green dots and dashes by the foliage. A party of men and women in evening clothes left the bar amid noise and hilarity. Everything appeared innocent and above-board.

Darrell walked slowly down the street across from the hotel. The parked cars were empty, no one lurked in doorways. He returned to the Mercedes-Benz.

The seat was vacant.

From the shadows came Ellen's voice. "Here I am." She stepped forward.

"You gave me a scare," said Darrell. "For a moment I thought…Well, never mind. The coast is clear. Let's go."

CHAPTER XV

THE NEXT DAY BEGAN placidly and quietly. Darrell and Ellen visited the United States consul, filled out several forms, and were asked to return after they were married.

They left the consulate, walked to the car, which had been parked in the Soco Grande. Ellen stroked the front fender. "Poor Mr. Burdette. I should have returned his car long ago."

"We'll let him have it this afternoon," said Darrell.

Ellen crossed the sidewalk to a newspaper kiosk, read the face of one of Tangier's Spanish newspapers. "Here's news about Noel."

Darrell bought the newspaper. "What does it say?"

"Not too much. 'Noel Hutson, American citizen, resident of Tangier, yesterday was found dead near Erfoud, village in the Tafilelt, over the Atlas. He had been driving a truck, presumably carrying contraband arms to the Algerian rebels, and had been killed by a shot through the heart.'"

"What's this?" asked Darrell. "A shot through the heart?"

"That's what it says here. You didn't see?"

"No. I just glanced in the cab. Strange. Go on."

" 'The cadaver was discovered in a truck concealed a short distance off the Ksar-es-Souk–Erfoud highway. The truck is registered to the Europe–Africa Transfer Society Anonymous'— that means corporation — 'of Tangier.

" 'Tangier officials, as well as important Rabat authorities, are investigating the death. It would be very disturbing to current sensitive French–Moroccan negotiations if a new contraband weapon-delivery system were found to be operating under the noses of the authorities.

The French would undoubtedly harden their attitude toward King Mohammed's representations that French troops leave Moroccan soil.

" 'Knowledgeable students of the situation will remember'—" Ellen stopped, looked down the column. "That's all there is. They go on about the French seizure of the *Slovenija* a while back. They don't mention us at all."

"I'm just as pleased." Darrell opened the door of the car for Ellen. "You drive, and I'll look at you."

"Darrell, you idiot. I'm not that nice to look at."

"Of course you are. Nicer. If we didn't have so many errands —"

"But we do." Ellen started the motor, drove to the police headquarters. Captain Goulidja informed Darrell that Noel's body had been brought to Tangier and now lay in the city morgue. He verified that Noel had been shot through the heart.

"That should simplify matters for you," mused Darrell.

"Why is this?"

"It means that whoever killed Noel did not shoot him from the road, or from the running-board — the bullet hole would be in Noel's head. Noel must have stopped the truck, come down from the cab. Under the circumstances he would have done so only for someone he trusted, someone he expected to see. Or someone he wasn't afraid of."

"Yes. That's quite possible." Captain Goulidja did not seem to consider the matter significant. "This afternoon, if you desire, we will release the body to your undertaker."

Darrell did so desire, and from the police headquarters went to the black marble office of an undertaker, where he made the necessary arrangements.

The time now was two o'clock. Darrell and Ellen ate a sandwich at an ice cream parlor, walked three blocks to the auctioneer's office and spent a lively period arguing with the auctioneer. He protested that the articles Ellen wished to withhold from sale were the only ones worth selling. Ellen retorted that the sale was not being arranged for the auctioneer's benefit; he in his turn pointed out that he had his own interests to consider, and that hawking a cupboardful of pots and pans, a few old tables and floor lamps was not his idea of a dignified livelihood. Eventually the contract was signed, and they went to the American

Express to arrange for the packing and shipment of the articles Ellen had retained: a grand piano, a grandfather clock, books, silver, a few pieces of Chinese porcelain, two Persian rugs.

Ellen was taken aback at the shipping charges. "Darrell!" she whispered. "That's more than all the other things will sell for!"

"So what? We'll have a piano and a clock and some rugs. We'll build a house around them. What do you think of that?"

"It's very nice, but am I worth all this money?"

Darrell assured her that a pedigreed sheep, in good health, sometimes brought even more.

They returned to the car. "Where now?" Ellen asked.

"Anywhere you like."

Ellen drove aimlessly through the streets.

"I shouldn't feel so happy and carefree," said Darrell presently. "It's hardly decent with poor Noel lying in the morgue."

"And you're really not interested in who killed him?"

Darrell laughed hollowly. "Abd Allah el Kazim wondered about that too. Of course I'm interested. It's been on my mind ever since we found him. It must have been someone he considered harmless, otherwise he never would have stopped. Remember, he's carrying all this heroin. He's scared, anxious, suspicious. Last night he tried three times to call Arthur Upshaw, but only made contact with X — Mr. or Mrs. or Miss, as the case may be. X promised to deliver a message to Arthur Upshaw, but Upshaw never calls back. What is Noel thinking? He wonders, did Upshaw get my message? If not, why not? Suppose X failed to deliver it? But why should X not deliver the message? When Noel comes up that slope he's got X on his mind. Lo and behold! Here stands X flagging him down. Noel can either stop or drive on past like the wind. He stops. Why? It must either be someone he considers innocuous, or someone he thinks is entitled to the heroin. In either case Noel sees X with pleasure and relief. He's glad to get rid of the heroin, he's glad to have company back to Tangier. Unluckily X shoots him. This was a month ago. The X's — Mr. X and Mrs., or Miss X — are sitting tight, waiting for the commotion to die before cashing in.

"I eliminate you from suspicion, for reasons already stated, also because I know you couldn't do such a thing. Arthur is the person for whom Noel would stop most readily. He seems perturbed and distressed — is he putting on an act? Duff, Ventriss, Jilali — all more or less possible. Perhaps some of them have alibis. If so the situation narrows even more. So that's it. What do you think?"

Ellen shook her head rather dismally. "I don't know. Your reasoning is certainly impressive. But there's still one matter you haven't accounted for."

"What?"

"Noel wrote you he was coppering his bets. How?"

"That I don't know," said Darrell. "No doubt we'll learn eventually."

They returned to the hotel. The clerk had a message for Darrell. "A lady has telephoned for you, Mr. Hutson. I told her you were not in."

"A lady? Did she leave her name?"

"No, sir. She said she would call again."

"I see."

Ellen went to her room; a few minutes later Darrell knocked at her door, and was admitted. She had changed into a pale blue suit; her tawny hair was brushed smooth and glistening.

"What about a drink before dinner?" Darrell proposed.

"I'll be ready in ten seconds."

"A lady has been telephoning me," said Darrell.

"Really? Who? Mrs. X?"

"I don't know. Perhaps someone from the undertaker's office. Shall we go across to the Masquerade, in case she calls back?"

Ellen hesitated. "We might see Duff and Arthur."

"If they have the nerve to show their faces, I have nerve enough to look at them."

Ellen laughed rather weakly. "When you put it that way, I do too."

Darrell stopped by the desk on their way out. "If the lady telephones again," he told the clerk, "I'll be over in the Masquerade."

"Very well, sir."

They crossed the street, pushed through the doors. Ellen stiffened. Arthur Upshaw and Duff sat in a booth. Upshaw watched them without expression, Duff scowled and ran his fingers through his already untidy hair.

Darrell stopped short, anger beginning to rise in him. Ellen took his arm, led him to the bar.

"Good evening, folks," said Phil Beresford. "What'll it be? Make it good, because there's just three more days."

Darrell ordered martinis. Mr. Burdette, sitting on his usual stool, waved a stern finger at Ellen. "Well, young lady. It's about time you were showing your face. I've got business to discuss with you."

"Yes, Mr. Burdette. It's parked outside. You can have it now." She offered him the keys.

Mr. Burdette held up his hands in plaintive dismay. "But I'm driving a demonstrator; what in the world will I do with two cars?"

"Would you like me to bring it in tomorrow morning?"

"Excellent. Please, please drive carefully tonight."

Phil served the drinks. "Incidentally, Mr. Hutson, the roving reporter wants to talk to you."

Darrell laughed uneasily, conscious of Ellen beside him. "She squeezed me dry last night."

"I'll call her down anyway. T-Bone makes things hum." He beckoned to his waiter. "Charley! Go call T-Bone, tell her that the place is in an uproar. Mr. Burdette's drunk and giving away big boxes of chocolate bonbons."

Mr. Burdette rubbed his plump face. "Saturday's your last night, Phil?"

"That's right, Mr. Burdette. Kinda hate to go."

"I assume that the house buys all day Saturday?"

"All day Sunday, and Monday too."

T-Bone appeared, halted at the sight of Ellen, then came forward. She looked at Mr. Burdette, then wrinkled her nose at Phil. "He's not giving away boxes of bonbons."

Mr. Burdette said, "I've got something else you can have."

"Quiet, Mr. Burdette," said Phil. "That kind of talk draws Mama out here. I'd hate to see you lose out on all those snacks."

T-Bone slid up on a stool beside Darrell. "Good evening, Mr. Hutson."

"Good evening, T-Bone."

"Is there anything new about Noel?"

"Nothing I know of."

"Do the police know who shot him?"

"If they do, they haven't told me."

"What a shame," said T-Bone. "Noel was such a nice boy. I was in love with him, wasn't I, Phil?"

Phil scratched his head. "I forget. Which day was it?"

"Aren't you ever serious, Phil?"

"You act on me like strong drink, T-Bone. Speaking of drink, since nobody's buying, I guess I'll pour one for myself." He mixed himself a highball. "Next time Mr. Burdette orders he'll only get half a jigger."

Mr. Burdette looked at him quizzically. "For a man who's being driven from business, you seem in the best of spirits."

"Laughing to keep from crying, Mr. Burdette."

T-Bone turned to Darrell. "What will you do with Noel's boat?"

"Nothing. Do you want it?"

T-Bone laughed delightedly. "Can I really have it?"

"Certainly."

"Shall I take it, Phil?"

"Take anything that's free."

"Will you help me paint it?"

"If you'll wear your bikini."

"This is a party I'd like to be in on," said Mr. Burdette.

Phil shook his head. "When T-Bone and I get busy painting we don't like to be disturbed." He looked over his shoulder, clapped his hand to his mouth.

Mrs. Phil came forward, looking neither right nor left. She muttered to Phil, turned, wheeled back into the kitchen. Phil turned to Darrell. "Telephone call. Take it in the booth."

Darrell told Ellen, "Must be the mysterious lady. Order us another drink." He slid off the stool, crossed the room, passing in front of Arthur Upshaw and Duff. They sat with heads averted.

He entered the booth, closed the door, picked up the receiver. "Darrell Hutson here."

"Hello. Mr. Hutson?"

"Yes, this is Mr. Hutson."

"This is Mrs. Ritterman from the hotel."

"Oh yes, Mrs. Ritterman."

"I saw in the newspapers about Noel. It is too bad. He was a nice boy. I am very sorry."

"Yes. I'm sorry too."

"He has his things here. His clothes."

"Will the clothes fit your husband? If they do —"

"Clothes from a dead man? No, never! And he has those two packages. He asked me to store them. These he said I must tell nobody. But now he is dead."

Darrell forced himself to speak casually. "What packages are these?"

"He sent me a letter about packages he is sending me to keep for him, in case he is not here. My husband has put them in the basement."

"How long ago was this?"

"After Noel left — a few days."

"I see. That's very interesting. Don't say anything about this to anyone else, please."

"Don't tell anyone?"

"No. There'll be somebody to pick them up tonight or tomorrow."

"Very well. I will wait."

"Thank you for calling, Mrs. Ritterman."

"I called because I saw in the papers about Noel. Terrible! The things they do!"

"Yes, it's a bad situation. Thanks again for calling."

Darrell hung up the receiver. He opened the door, stood looking across the room. Ellen watched curiously from the bar; Arthur Upshaw and Duff peered from under their eyebrows... Noel had coppered his bets. He had sent the heroin ahead as a precaution. His thoughts, his fears, his motives, his plans were all revealed. Sitting in the lonely lobby of the Gîte d'Etape he had evolved his scheme:

"...Wire the money care of the Lombard Bank at Tangier. I'll collect if and when I get there.

"I just figured a way to copper my bets, and I'm safe as far as Tangier. I may have to do some fast talking..."

So Noel had written. The next morning he had driven into Erfoud and mailed the heroin to Mrs. Ritterman.

He had coppered his bets — or so he believed.

Someone had given Noel no chance to do his fast talking, no chance to explain. Someone had killed Noel without asking.

Without asking? But Noel had been shot in the chest. Had someone asked, then fired the shot? Perplexity.

Ellen was watching him with growing puzzlement. Darrell started back across the room. Arthur Upshaw glanced up as he passed. Darrell stopped, looked down, skin crawling with detestation. In a strained metallic voice he said, "You two have a lot of gall showing your faces."

Arthur Upshaw sat impassively. Duff blurted, "She killed your brother, you stupid fool! She killed your brother, she ripped us up the back!"

"Ellen didn't take your heroin, Duff."

Duff laughed savagely. "She can talk sweet when she wants to. She's making a fool of you!"

Darrell shook his head, feeling the beginnings of a great content. "You saw me take a phone call? Ellen never had your heroin. I just found out where it is. In ten minutes I could put my hands on it."

"Where?" The word burst up out of Upshaw like a belch.

Darrell laughed. "Read about it in tomorrow's newspapers. Excuse me. I've got some thinking to do."

Darrell returned to his seat. Ellen asked, "Who was the lady?"

"Mrs. Ritterman from Noel's hotel. She wanted to know what to do with Noel's belongings." He squeezed her hand. "Excuse me a minute. I've got to think. I'm on the track of something."

"More theories?"

"Yes. Perhaps the right ones this time. My last were way off base." He sat looking into his glass. Noise flowed around him unheard — chatter and laughter, the clink of glass and ice, the jingle of the cash-register, the tapping of Ellen playing with her car keys.

Phil amiably bickered with Mr. Burdette: "You mean to say there's women more beautiful than T-Bone? You name one, I'll eat her. If I can catch her."

"Well, consider Helen of Troy."

"No comparison. They built 'em big and beefy in those days, not cute like T-Bone."

"What? The face that launched a thousand ships?"

"T-Bone's lunched with a thousand rips. That's not counting the dinners." He pinched her cheek.

"Phil! Be-*have* yourself! Psst, here's Mrs. Phil."

Mrs. Phil sailed past with a cold glare for T-Bone. "Telephone," she told Mr. Burdette gruffly, swung around, marched back the way she had come. Mr. Burdette slipped his round haunch off the bar-stool, vanished into the kitchen.

Phil shook his head. "It ain't right. I get a dirty look for checking T-Bone's tonsils, but Mama carries on like billy-o with Mr. Burdette in the kitchen. She claims it's the telephone, but she's feeding him lamb-chops with both hands. I'm gonna get that telephone moved out of the kitchen, so I'll know what's going on around here."

Someone tapped Darrell's shoulder. Darrell looked around, Arthur Upshaw loomed over him. "I want to talk with you. I've got a proposition you may be interested in."

"Forget your proposition, Mr. Upshaw."

"Don't make a fool of yourself, Hutson," said Arthur Upshaw in a menacing voice. "This matter is not your concern. Keep out of it."

"But it is. My brother was killed. And in about two minutes I'm going to call the police and tell them all about it."

"Tell them all about what?"

"Where they can find the heroin. Where they can come for the man who killed Noel."

"Tell me, tell me!" squealed T-Bone. "I want to know!"

Darrell twisted the stem of his glass. Five faces watched him. The group stood or sat at the end of the bar, out of earshot of the other patrons.

"Very well," said Darrell. "I'll tell you. I'll tell all of you. It's no mystery — now. Five minutes ago I learned that on the morning of the day Noel was killed, he mailed two packages to Tangier."

Arthur Upshaw and Duff leaned forward, their eyes burning down at Darrell. "Go on," Arthur Upshaw grated.

"Do I need to? Isn't it clear what happened? Somebody outside your organization killed Noel. Call him Mr. X. Neither you nor Duff nor anyone else associated with you would shoot Noel under these circumstances; you'd be too anxious to get your dope back again. But Mr. X went south in the middle of the night. He stopped Noel. There was nothing aboard the truck. No heroin. Mr. X shot Noel anyway, to keep tales from being carried back to Tangier." Darrell paused, sipped his highball. "So now the question: who is Mr. X?"

He looked around the group. Five pairs of eyes watched him.

"Go on," said Arthur Upshaw.

"Noel made three calls from Erfoud to Tangier."

"No," exclaimed Duff. "Two calls!"

"Three calls. The first to the Balmoral. Aktouf told him Mr. Upshaw was not in. Then Noel called the McKinstry house. No answer. On the third call he spoke to Mr. X. Noel was excited. He probably made it pretty clear what he was carrying — or refusing to carry. Mr. X drove south. He shot Noel. But no loot. Mr. X was furious. Also Mrs. X — or Miss X. There was a lady along too. All the work for nothing. The long drive, the killing, now the drive back. They must have been very disappointed. They drove the truck out in the desert, turned it down the gully, returned to Tangier."

"So much is clear," rasped Arthur Upshaw. "Who are these two people?"

"Where would Noel make a third call hoping to find you? Why not here, at the Masquerade Bar?"

Arthur Upshaw looked at Phil. Duff looked at Phil. Darrell looked at Phil. Phil drew back, looking from face to face. "Here, here, here. What's all this?"

"The call came to you," said Darrell. "Where else?"

"You're out of your mind!" cried Phil. "You think I ranted down there and shot Noel? You've lost your wits!"

"You own a sports car — an MG. No Mercedes-Benz, but something similar at a casual glance."

Phil leaned against the back counter, face twisted and wry. "Darrell, I give you credit for more sense. Look at me here in this bar. I haven't had a night off in a year. Anybody can tell you that. Ask Mr. Burdette. Ask T-Bone. You think I could leave here at two in the morning, halfgassed as I usually am, and make the trip to Erfoud? That's wild!"

Darrell hesitated. "You might have flown down."

"In my private airplane which I don't have? On a broomstick? Your reasoning is full of prunes. Take it from me, no such telephone call came here. If my word's not good enough, ask Mama. She takes all the telephone calls around here. She'll tell you. We'll settle this right now." He went to the door, looked into the kitchen. "Hey, Mama, come out here a minute. Hey, Mama!"

Phil leaned forward, went out into the kitchen. Duff walked quickly after him. They heard Phil's voice: "Mama!"

Phil came back, his face long and dubious. "Mama's gone goodbye. Mr. Burdette too. Unless they're eating somewhere on the sly."

Something popped inside Darrell's head. He felt as if ice water were trickling down his back. "Mama listens in on telephone calls?"

"I'm sorry to say she does."

"Then she heard Mrs. Ritterman call me."

"Ritterman!" bawled Duff. "That's the Hotel de los Dos Continentes. Noel's hotel. That's where the stuff is! Come on!"

"Call a cab!" bellowed Arthur.

Duff snatched the keys from Ellen's fingers. "We'll take the Mercedes!" They ran from the bar.

Phil stood holding his head with his hands. "This is wrong! This is one of T-Bone's fables. This can't be. Not nice Mr. Burdette and Mama. Somebody wake me from this bad dream."

"He's got a whole agency full of sports cars," said Ellen.

Phil came out from behind the bar. "We can't just stand here. Let's go! This is a gala event! It's so pathetic it's funny. Arthur and Duff chasing Mama and Mr. Burdette."

"What have they done?" cried T-Bone. "Won't somebody tell me?"

"I've got to call the police," said Darrell.

"I'll call them," said Ellen. "I can do it faster." She ran to the phone booth.

"If you're coming, come," cried Phil, ignoring the stares of his patrons. "They got a big head-start!"

T-Bone tugged at his arm. "I want to come too."

"You call your newspapers! There's a hundred thousand francs in it. This is big-time!"

T-Bone hesitated, then ran to the phone booth. She rattled the door.

Ellen came out; T-Bone darted in, darted back out. "Phil! I don't have any money!"

"Get it out of the cash register! I can't wait!"

"But I don't know what to tell them! I don't know what's happened!"

"Tell 'em the unhappy truth: that Mama and Mr. Burdette massacred poor Noel Hutson!"

Darrell and Ellen piled into the MG; Phil started the motor, made a hard U-turn; they roared down the hill. From another direction came the sound of a siren. "We'll never catch them," groaned Phil. "To think I should see the day!"

"Well, I made a fool of myself," said Darrell dourly. "While I was theorizing, they were loading heroin into their car."

"You were pretty close at that," said Phil. "I don't blame you."

They crossed the Boulevard Pasteur, twisted left down the hill, bounced into the Calle Erasmus. Mrs. Ritterman stood in the doorway, looking up and down in bewilderment. She saw Darrell and asked hopefully, "You sent them for the packages, Mr. Hutson? It was right, yes?"

"Where did they go?" cried Phil.

"Down there." She pointed along the street. "Just one minute ago. And another car too. One minute ago!"

Behind came the sound of a siren, loud and shrill. The MG spun forward. "They must have turned down to the water-front. That's the only place this street takes you. Hang on! My, my! I'm really surprised. Mr. Burdette, so meek and quiet. Mama must have fed him awful strong meat."

They turned sharp right, bounded over a vacant lot. "Short-cut," Phil explained. "We gain two blocks on them."

They bumped across the sidewalk, swung out upon the water-front highway.

A quarter-mile ahead appeared a small spark, a quick burst of poppy-colored flame.

Ellen gasped. Phil clicked his tongue against his teeth. "That looks bad."

The orange flame rolled and seethed, became a ball, heavy as honey, scrolled with black smoke. Phil pulled up to within two hundred feet, parked, jumped out. A gasoline truck lay twisted across the road. Underneath, revealed through fitful gaps in the flame, lay the smashed hulk of a sports car. Two dull black humps, anonymous as pillows, could be glimpsed.

A crowd had already gathered. Several cars had halted. Ahead was the Mercedes-Benz. Arthur Upshaw and Duff stood staring into the flames, Upshaw making little running movements forward, then drawing back. Behind, a police car screamed to a halt. Three white-uniformed troopers sprang out, ran toward the blaze, stopped helplessly.

Phil turned back to the car. "I can't watch any more of this."

They drove slowly away, great billows of orange light reflected in the windshield. Phil heaved a deep sigh. "I feel kinda sad. Poor Mama. Poor Mr. Burdette. The world has just come to an end for them…Gives a man a funny feeling."

CHAPTER XVI

PHIL PARKED IN FRONT of the Masquerade. The three alighted. T-Bone came running from the bar. "What happened, Phil? Where have you been?"

Phil put his arm limply around her shoulders. "We've been chasing Mama and Mr. Burdette, T-Bone. We chased and chased till the chase came to an end."

"But what happened? Where are they?"

"They're dead. Ran into a gasoline truck, probably doing eighty or ninety."

"Phil! Not really!"

"Really and truly. This very minute Mama's feeding Mr. Burdette ambrosia sandwiches. Or more likely, a brimstone milkshake."

T-Bone put her head against Phil's shoulder; he patted her hair. "Don't feel sorry, T-Bone — not for me. You know how things were."

"I know, but —"

He nodded. "It's a shock when things blow up so sudden. Come on, Darrell, Ellen. Let's go have a drink." He took T-Bone's arm, walked with her into the bar. Darrell and Ellen followed. Their glasses remained where they had left them; at Mr. Burdette's place a lonely highball waited, the last fragment of ice floating at the surface. Phil ducked behind the bar, snatched the glass, started to empty it, then halted. He went into the kitchen, returned with an African violet blossom. He dropped it into the highball, set the little bouquet on top of the cash register. "In reverence to Mr. Burdette and Mama," said Phil. "Murderers and villains though they may be."

He looked around the room. It was the dinner hour, the bar was almost empty. A few faces looked back. Phil beckoned to the waiter. "Charley, go lock up. Bar is closed for the night. No more drinks."

Arthur Upshaw and Duff pushed in before Charley reached the door. Arthur Upshaw's skin was tight over his bones, his eyes blazed. He walked over to the bar, glared down at Darrell. "Do you understand the cost of your interference? Four hundred thousand pounds of my money!"

"A big shipment of heroin has been destroyed," said Darrell. "Isn't that what you mean?"

Upshaw abruptly swung toward Phil. "Give me a double whiskey."

"Bar is closed, Mr. Upshaw. I'm not serving tonight."

Arthur Upshaw strode into the Balmoral lobby. Duff hesitated, looked down at Ellen. "I'm sorry about yesterday. I'm really sorry, Ellen."

Ellen turned her head. Duff shrugged. He tossed the car keys upon the bar, followed Upshaw.

Phil set two bottles of whiskey on the bar. "Drinks is on the house. A shame Mr. Burdette can't be here to enjoy it. But that's the way things go."

"I don't understand any of this," T-Bone complained.

Phil, pouring highballs, shook his head. "I don't understand too much myself."

"But what happened, Phil?"

"Well, near as I can see it, Mr. Burdette and Mama thought they needed some extra money. They didn't quite make the grade and shot Noel Hutson out of vexation."

"But Mr. Burdette and Mama!"

"Yes, T-Bone, it's a shock." He swallowed two-thirds of his highball. "But one thing I've learned in my years on this earth: you never know what's going on in someone else's mind." He looked at her fixedly.

"Stop that, Phil!" T-Bone wriggled on the bar stool. "You make me feel all funny."

Phil finished his highball, set the glass down with a rap. "Yep. This is a funny business, this life thing. I haven't quite got it figured. Darrell, drink up. This is a momentous night. Chances are I'll get a little gassed. Ellen, drink up. It's a farewell party. For Noel and Mama and Mr. Burdette." He mixed himself another highball, raised the glass. "Hail and farewell." He signaled the waiter. "Charley. Start turning out the lights. Chase these people out of here."

Phil replenished glasses. "This is the right way to hold a wake, with a well-stocked saloon to roam around in. T-Bone, dip your beak. It's free."

"I don't like whiskey very much."

"Throw it out, I'll mix you a real drink. A French .75 — champagne and cognac. There, how's that?"

"It's nice," said T-Bone. "But I don't have time to drink it." She looked toward the Balmoral lobby. "I've got to go dress."

"Dress? What for? You're dressed."

"I've got a date for dinner."

"That was before you became my new fiancée."

T-Bone laughed uneasily. "How can I be your fiancée, Phil?"

"It's got to be done, T-Bone. I can't smuggle you into the States unless I marry you." He shot a cautious glance over his shoulder toward the kitchen. "Confound it! I got myself into a mean habit."

"Phil, won't you ever be serious!"

"I'm utterly serious. I'm on my way to the States. If you want to come, you better start packing your trousseau."

T-Bone bent her head over her glass. "Where in the States?"

"New York. Beverly Hills. Honolulu. I don't know for sure."

"I have a friend in Hollywood," said T-Bone thoughtfully. "He promised me a screen test."

Phil put his knuckle under her chin, raised her head. "Does that mean yes or no?"

"Yes or no what?"

"Are you coming with me to the States?"

"Then you're really leaving?"

"Certainly I'm leaving. Do you think I want to stay here?" He poured himself a whiskey with a lavish hand. "We'll settle this matter now. T-Bone, look me in the eye. Repeat after me: 'I —'"

T-Bone jumped off the stool. "Phil, I can't stay another minute. Mr. Sverdlup will be here, and I haven't even had my bath." She patted his hand.

"T-Bone! Are you my fiancée or not?"

"I promised Mr. Sverdlup —"

"T-Bone! Yes or no?"

"Yes, but —"

"But what?"

"Nothing."

"Repeat after me: 'Mr. Sverdlup, go chase yourself.'"

"No, Phil, I couldn't do that. He's very nice and now —"

"T-Bone! Look me in the eye. Say, 'I love you madly.'"

"I love you madly."

"That's better. You've made me a happy man, T-Bone." He raised his glass. "To our new lives!"

They drank, and T-Bone departed for her dinner engagement.

Phil locked the door behind her. "If I got any brains I'll leave early tomorrow morning before T-Bone remembers she wants to go to Hollywood. I suppose I could always claim I was drunk." The bar was now almost empty. Phil poured out whiskey, soda, cognac, champagne indiscriminately. "Another toast. The memory of Noel, Mr. Burdette and Mama!"

Ellen laughed sadly. "That's a unique toast. The murderers and the victim in the same breath."

"Yeah," said Phil. "I guess it's not generally done." He went to the cash register, took the half-filled highball glass with the floating African violet, poured it slowly into the sink. "Farewell, Mama. Farewell, Mr. Burdette. In spite of your sins in life, I wish you luck."

He dropped the glass into the waste barrel.

Darrell and Ellen got down off the bar stools. "Come along, Phil," said Darrell. "Let's go get a bite to eat."

"Right," said Phil. "It's too sad hanging around here. I'll be with you, soon as I clean out the cash register."

"We'll wait in front."

They stood out under the green light of the sign. A click. The light died as the sign went out. The street seemed barren and colorless.

A few minutes later Phil joined them, and they walked down the hill toward the Place de France.

JACK VANCE was born in 1916 to a well-off California family that, as his childhood ended, fell upon hard times. As a young man he worked at a series of unsatisfying jobs before studying mining engineering, physics, journalism and English at the University of California Berkeley. Leaving school as America was going to war, he found a place as an ordinary seaman in the merchant marine. Later he worked as a rigger, surveyor, ceramicist, and carpenter before his steady production of sf, mystery novels, and short stories established him as a full-time writer.

His output over more than sixty years was prodigious and won him three Hugo Awards, a Nebula Award, a World Fantasy Award for lifetime achievement, as well as an Edgar from the Mystery Writers of America. The Science Fiction and Fantasy Writers of America named him a grandmaster and he was inducted into the Science Fiction Hall of Fame.

His works crossed genre boundaries, from dark fantasies (including the highly influential *Dying Earth* cycle of novels) to interstellar space operas, from heroic fantasy (the *Lyonesse* trilogy) to murder mysteries featuring a sheriff (the Joe Bain novels) in a rural California county. A Vance story often centered on a competent male protagonist thrust into a dangerous, evolving situation on a planet where adventure was his daily fare, or featured a young person setting out on a perilous odyssey over difficult terrain populated by entrenched, scheming enemies.

Late in his life, a world-spanning assemblage of Vance aficionados came together to return his works to their original form, restoring material cut by editors whose chief preoccupation was the page count of a pulp magazine. The result was the complete and authoritative *Vance Integral Edition* in 44 hardcover volumes. Spatterlight Press is now publishing the VIE texts as ebooks, and as print-on-demand paperbacks.

Colophon

This book was printed using Adobe Arno Pro as the primary text font, with NeutraFace used on the cover.

This title was created from the digital archive of the Vance Integral Edition, a series of 44 books produced under the aegis of the author by a worldwide group of his readers. The VIE project gratefully acknowledges the editorial guidance of Norma Vance, as well as the cooperation of the Department of Special Collections at Boston University, whose John Holbrook Vance collection has been an important source of textual evidence.

Special thanks to R.C. Lacovara, Patrick Dusoulier, Koen Vyverman, Paul Rhoads, Chuck King, Gregory Hansen, Suan Yong, and Josh Geller for their invaluable assistance preparing final versions of the source files.

Source: Mike Berro, Koen Vyverman; Digitize: Mark Adams, Richard Chandler, Richard White, Dave Worden; Diff: Hans van der Veeke, Suan Hsi Yong; Diff-Merge: Steve Sherman; Tech Proof: Suan Hsi Yong; Text Integrity: Patrick Dusoulier, Paul Rhoads, Tim Stretton, Suan Hsi Yong; Implement: Derek W. Benson, Hans van der Veeke; Security: Paul Rhoads, Tim Stretton; Compose: John A. Schwab; Comp Review: Marcel van Genderen, Charles King, Bob Luckin; Update Verify: John A. D. Foley, Bob Luckin, Paul Rhoads; RTF-Diff: Patrick Dusoulier, Charles King; Textport: Patrick Dusoulier; Proofread: Erik Arendse, Patrick Dusoulier, Rob Gerrand, Ed Gooding, Marc Herant, Karl Kellar, David A. Kennedy, Bob Luckin, Jim Pattison, Linda Petersen, Joel Riedesel, David White

Artwork (maps based on original drawings by Jack and Norma Vance):

Paul Rhoads, Christopher Wood

Book Composition and Typesetting: Joel Anderson

Art Direction and Cover Design: Howard Kistler

Proofing: Steve Sherman, Dave Worden

Jacket Blurb: John Vance

Management: John Vance, Koen Vyverman

www.ingramcontent.com/pod-product-compliance
Lightning Source LLC
Chambersburg PA
CBHW020635180626
46816CB00003B/974